A NOVEL BASED ON
THE MAJOR MOTION PICTURE

A NOVEL BASED ON
THE MAJOR MOTION PICTURE

Screenplay by Robert Rodriguez
Adapted by Kitty Richards

miramax books

HYPERION BOOKS FOR CHILDREN
NEW YORK

Printed in the United States of America
First Edition
1 3 5 7 9 10 8 6 4 2

ISBN 0-7868-1762-3

Library of Congress Catalog Card Number on file.

A NOVEL BASED ON
THE MAJOR MOTION PICTURE

CHAPTER 1

Agua Park was deserted. All the pools—Tidal Waves of Terror, Rolling Rapids, even Kiddie Korner—were drained. The sky was gray, and a chill wind blew dry leaves across the empty park. Ex–OSS Level One Secret Agent, now private detective, Juni Cortez shivered and drew the collar of his very stylin' trench coat closed. He was on the job, pounding the pavement, solving a case. His going rate was $4.99 an hour. Plus expenses.

His eyes scanned the empty water park. Then he turned to face his client. "I know why the water from your park is missing," he said to her.

"Pray tell," she replied.

"It's winter. They shut down the park during the winter," Juni explained.

"Who's *they*?" the girl wanted to know.

"The people who really own this park," Juni answered.

Case closed.

◎ ◎ ◎

Up in his tree house, Juni counted his cash yet again and shoved it into his piggy bank. He sighed.

"Times are tough, and a guy's gotta do what a guy's gotta do," he said to himself. He sat back and recalled some of the cases he had solved. Lost hamsters. Unfaithful best friends. Missing lunch money.

Brrrring! Juni grabbed his cell phone. "OSS?" he said. "Oh, brother." He took a deep breath. "Look, I'm no longer an agent," he explained. "I can't help you. Whatever it is, it's your problem. Leave me alone."

He hung up his phone and stuck even more money into his bank. His hard work was paying off. Juni was saving up for something big, and he had just about enough money.

◎ ◎ ◎

With his piggy bank tucked safely under his arm, Juni waited patiently in line. He watched with interest as a TV in the window announced: *"The biggest video game to ever be created, period. This is a worldwide event. The game was created by some-*

one known only as . . . the Toymaker, who was, once again, unavailable for interviews."

Juni, along with what seemed like every other kid in the universe, was lined up to buy his copy of the biggest virtual-reality game in history—GAME OVER. It was going online at midnight.

Already starting to get bored, he glanced through the window of a charity office next door. A man in a wheelchair was washing the windows. Juni glanced down at his necklace, a gift from his grandfather, Valentin.

It gave him an idea. Maybe there were more important things in life than video games. He left the line and began to walk toward the charity office. But a game seller with a bullhorn began to shout, it seemed, almost to Juni himself. "Oh, and did we mention the surprises the Toymaker has in store for all those who complete Level Five?" he thundered. "Untold riches. Toys and prizes beyond your wildest dreams . . ."

Untold riches! Juni turned and tried to get back into the line.

"Hey, no cutting in line, freak," a kid said with a scowl.

"I'm not cutting," Juni protested. "I was standing right here. . . ."

"End of the line!" another kid shouted.

"End of the line!" everyone echoed.

Juni looked up. The end of the line was at least two blocks away. He sighed and began to trudge to the end. At the corner, not looking where he was going, he tripped on the curb, and dropped his piggy bank. It shattered into hundreds of pieces. Pennies, nickels, dimes, quarters, and silver dollars rolled every which way. Juni looked up and watched his paper money flying off into the sky.

The kids' laughter echoing in his ears, Juni watched the last of his hard-earned money disappear in a puff of wind.

Figures, he thought. Things had been pretty lame for him since he left the OSS.

Well, at least things can't get any worse, Juni mused to himself.

He had no idea how wrong he was.

CHAPTER 2

At home, Juni sat by the window, holding the necklace that his grandfather had given to him. The necklace was a reminder that his grandfather was always thinking of him. On a nearby table, the family photos were displayed. Juni looked at a photo of his grandfather on the table, and then picked up a postcard from his parents. On the front Ingrid and Gregorio were skydiving. *Wish you could be here!* the postcard read. *We'll be done with this mission later in the week! As always, call if you need anything, and we'll be right there. Make sure Thumb Thumb is charged up.*

Juni's Thumb Thumb valet sat in the kitchen reading the newspaper. On the refrigerator behind him were postcards from all of Carmen and his parents' missions—*We send our love!—See you in three days!—Call and we'll be there!—See you right after this mission!—See you tomorrow!—See you next Wednesday!*

Juni walked to the tree house. A package was waiting for him. It was from Romero, a wacky scientist Juni and Carmen had helped out on what turned out to be Juni's last case. Juni tore into the package eagerly. *Dear Juni,* the letter said. *I was doing some work and thought you might like these.* Inside was a fishbowl filled with miniature hammerhead and great white sharks. *Remember, they're still man-eaters, so don't be poking your fingers in the bowl,* Juni read just as he put his finger in the water. He yanked it out as three mini sharks leaped up—*SNAP! SNAP! SNAP!*—to take a bite. *Take care, and if you guys ever need anything, pick up the phone. I'll be there. Romero.*

Juni crumpled up the letter. "Yeah, yeah, okay," he said. While he was checking to make sure one of the mini sharks hadn't taken a mini bite out of his finger, Juni heard a familiar sound. The sound of propellers. Wanting to look preoccupied—hey, private eyes are *just* as busy as OSS agents—he quickly rearranged the papers on his desk.

"Spider? Ralph?" he called to his mini robots.

Ralph, a small spiderlike robot, plopped down on the desk in front of Juni.

"Where's Spider?" Juni wanted to know.

Ralph shrugged.

"Whatcha do with him, Ralph?" Juni asked.

Ralph shuffled to his feet, his arms behind his back.

"Write a thank-you note back to Romero," Juni commanded and began to dictate.

As Ralph wrote away, using a glow pen, Spider sneaked up on him from behind, brandishing a wooden pencil like a spear. Spider was a gift from Romero. He was a minature version of a combination creature—a spider and an ape. The top half was all ape and the bottom half was all spider.

Juni finished dictating. "'Signed, Juni Cortez,'" he said.

As Ralph completed the comma, Spider leaped right over him and scribbled Juni's name. The two mini robots had a competition thing going. A fierce one.

Ralph was furious! Spider did a victory dance, his pencil held high. He beat his chest in glee.

Ralph faced off, holding his glow pen like a light saber. Spider faced him, wielding the pencil. They lunged and parried.

"Behave, guys," said Juni, glancing at the fishbowl and the furiously snapping mini sharks. "You're upsetting the sharks."

Just then Spy Kid Agent Gerti Giggles flew in

the window, her propeller pigtails flying. She sat across the table from Juni.

"Whatcha doin'?" she asked.

"Hi, Gerti," said Juni. "I'm just doing . . . nothing," he admitted. "Again."

"Got any oldy moldy gadgets?" she asked.

Juni pulled out the spy paraphernalia that had served him and Carmen so well over the years, but that was now hopelessly out of date. Then he poured Gerti a thick, dark, sweet-smelling drink from a pitcher as she took inventory.

"Nano technology," Gerti said, reminiscing. "Remember those days?" She made a face. "Sheesh. Low tech." She sat down and noticed the drink Juni had poured. "What's that?"

"Mexican chocolate," Juni answered.

Gerti grinned and took the pitcher instead of the cup. She drank heartily.

"Where's your mom and dad?" she asked, putting the pitcher down. She sported a handsome Mexican chocolate mustache.

Juni reached into his pocket and chivalrously drew out a handkerchief. She took it and wiped her mouth.

"On assignment," he answered. "I could have gone, but I wanted to stay and finish up some work. It was my idea not to be part of the family business," he continued. "They were supportive. But now . . ."

"They're all on missions," Gerti finished for him. "Your sister too, huh?"

Juni nodded sadly. "I haven't seen Carmen since . . ." he thought for a moment. "Christmas. Last year."

Gerti leaned forward. "Does that upset you?"

"Yes." Juni answered. "No," he said after a pause.

Gerti played with the now empty pitcher of chocolate.

"Maybe so," Juni finished.

Gerti nodded. "You should sign back up. The OSS could really use you."

"Yeah," Juni said bitterly. "*Use* me."

Gerti shook her head impatiently. "Not what I meant. Don't hold on to the past, Juni. Look at me," she said proudly. "Nine years old, and nowhere to go but up."

Juni grew thoughtful. "Just seems more and more like the only tribe worth belonging to . . . is the one you're born into."

Gerti smiled. "Your family. It's good to take care of your family, Juni. But remember one thing . . . *everyone's* your family." She reached across the table, drained the cup of chocolate that Juni had poured, and flew out the window.

"Thanks for the gadgets!" she called as she left. "They'll fetch a hefty price at the OSS auction site."

Juni stared after her, deep in thought. He was puzzled. "What does she mean, *'everyone's* my family'? That makes no sense," he mumbled to himself.

Suddenly the window he was staring at became a computer screen. "Incoming call," the computer said.

"Hail to the Chief" began to play, and the presidential seal appeared on the screen. Yikes! Juni scrambled to look even busier than before.

"Hello, Juni," the president said, very presidentially.

"Mr. President," replied Juni.

"Oh, you can call me Devlin," the president of the United States answered.

Juni stared at the Chief Executive. He knew exactly what Devlin was up to. "What do you want, Mr. President? You know, you were already running the country when you were director of the OSS. This is sort of a step down, isn't it?"

"I *was* running the country," Devlin answered. "But since the OSS is a secret organization, no one knew it. I wanted the world to *know* that I'm in charge. So I became president of the United States. It depends on your preference. Reality or perception. Perception works for me."

"Well, Devlin . . ."—Juni corrected himself—"Mr. President. I'm into reality, and the reality is nothing you say will make me rejoin the OSS. That is why you called, is it not?"

"The OSS needs you to return," Devlin said.

"I'm retired," Juni said firmly.

"Ah, who's living in perception?" Devlin said. "Fact is, there's no retirement from the OSS. Once an agent, always an agent. And right now you need to be a big boy and go to the OSS and reinstate."

"With all due respect, sir," said Juni. "No."

Devlin sighed. "Well then, hold on to your seat because here's the reality." He paused. "Your sister is missing."

Juni's heart skipped a beat. Carmen—missing? He looked at her picture sitting on his desk.

This changed everything.

CHAPTER 3

$\rfloor$uni drove his pod boat right out of the water and up the front steps of the OSS headquarters. He leaped off, Ralph on one shoulder, Spider on the other.

"Cllciihj alkkdhfso ewoijhoi," said Ralph.

"I don't have my jet shoes," answered Juni. "I gave them to Gerti."

"OOO oo aagh aggh," retorted Spider.

"Thanks a lot," said Juni, totally offended.

Juni tossed his keys to the valet, took a deep breath, and stepped inside.

OSS headquarters was bustling with activity. But as soon as the agents recognized Juni they dropped everything and ran over to him. "Take Agent Cortez to Games and Theory!" the Processor commanded. A wheelie device appeared, and Juni hopped on.

"That's *ex*-Agent Cortez," Juni corrected.

"Fast! Fast! Fast!" shouted an agent. They reached a large, imposing, hexagon-shaped door.

"Through that door, agent. Quickly!" the agent commanded. "No time to lose!"

Juni scrambled into the room. The door slammed behind him. He looked around. The room was quiet and empty. There was one wall of cubicles, lined up as far as the eye could see. Another wall was a giant video screen. Suddenly several agents who had been blending into the wall stepped forward. They were eating doughnuts.

"We've been waiting for you," said Donnagon. The room suddenly came to life. Agents began entering their cubicles.

"Donnagon," replied Juni. "Been a good boy lately?" Juni hadn't seen Gerti's dad since he and Carmen had foiled Donnagon's plan to take over the world.

"Yes," Donnagon said quickly. "Very, very good. Step this way, please."

"Mrs. Giggles must have straightened you out," Juni observed.

"I certainly did," replied Mrs. Giggles, who had just stepped into the room. Juni could understand Donnagon's rapid turnaround. Mrs. Giggles was as tough as nails!

"Hello, Francesca," said Juni.

"Yeah, she worked me over pretty good there," admitted Donnagon.

Francesca, also known as Cesca, leaned forward. "So what do you know about a new video game called GAME OVER?" she asked Juni.

Juni furrowed his brow. "A little," he replied. "I know it goes online at midnight, and that just about every kid in the world is going to sign on and play."

Cesca shook her head firmly. "Not if we can help it. The game is a trap."

Donnagon joined in. "No one can actually win. In fact, everyone loses—their free will. Their mind basically gets taken over by the game."

"Once their kids are plugged in," Cesca continued, "parents won't be able to get their children's attention."

Juni was not impressed. "What else is new?" he scoffed.

"This is different," Cesca said. "Once a player gets through the game, the player's mind belongs to the Toymaker."

Juni's jaw dropped. "The Toymaker?" he said.

"The inventor of the game," explained Donnagon. "He intends to enslave the world's youth with mind control. If you control the youth . . . you control the future of the world."

An image of Carmen appeared on a nearby monitor. She was in the middle of a fight.

"She's an ingenious hacker, your sister," said Cesca admiringly. "We sent her inside to hack at the mainframe. She managed to install a virus that would trap the Toymaker within his own game. She almost succeeded in shutting down the entire system . . . but . . ."

"She disappeared," finished Donnagon.

Juni looked puzzled. "How could she disappear inside a game?"

"She didn't, physically," said Donnagon. "Actually, she's right here." He hit a button, and a screen rose, revealing a spherical room. Carmen floated in suspension, wearing goggles.

"Carmen!" Juni cried.

"She can't hear you," Cesca said. "Her mind is still in the game. She got as far as Level Four, then . . . nothing. She was the best chance we had."

Donnagon looked Juni straight in the eye. "And now we got you. Talk about downsizing . . ."

Cesca gripped her husband's neck tightly. "Darling? Behave," she said in a warning tone.

"Yes, sweetheart, of course," Donnagon said in a high voice.

Juni shook his head. This wasn't adding up. "Why me? I mean I don't get it. Why would she even go in there without any backup? She's too smart for that."

"Her first and only choice for backup wasn't available," said Cesca,

"Who?" asked Juni, his stomach sinking.

"You," replied Donnagon. "We tried several times to make contact but . . . we couldn't get through. She decided to go alone."

"You have to go in," said Cesca. "Find your sister, help her shut down the game in twelve hours. Or it's Game Over . . . for everyone."

Juni stood, deep in thought. He swore he'd never work for the OSS again. But Carmen was in trouble. She needed his help! There was only one thing to do.

"Are you with us?" Cesca asked.

Juni took a deep breath. "Okay," he said.

"Then let's go," she said.

CHAPTER 4

The OSS agents didn't waste a minute, suiting Juni up immediately and debriefing him the whole time with information for his entry into the game.

Juni was taking it all in. "So I have to shut down the game, but not release the Toymaker," he concluded.

"Exactly," said Cesca. "It would be catastrophic if he escaped. He's an evil mastermind. And he *hates* the OSS for imprisoning him in cyberspace."

Juni raised an eyebrow.

"You'll have to start on Level One like everyone else and make your way to Level Four, where you'll find your sister. Then proceed through Level Five," said Donnagon.

"Which is unwinnable," explained Cesca.

"Unwinnable?" Juni said in disbelief.

Donnagon nodded. "And that's where you shut

down the game. If it's not shut down, you'll be trapped inside with everyone else when the Toymaker takes over the world."

Juni took Ralph, then Spider, off his shoulders and carefully handed them to an agent. "Keep them apart," he warned. "They're still working out some issues."

Juni was strapped into a seat. *I can do this*, he said to himself.

"You'll find some humans in the game," Cesca explained. "Beta testers are expert gamers from around the world, let in first to try the game. If you can earn their trust, they might help you."

"Then there are the programmerz. They wrote the security codes and guard the game. They *won't* help you. Got it?" said Donnagon.

"Uh, yeah," said Juni.

The seat moved forward, then halted directly in front of two closed doors. A watch was strapped on Juni's wrist. He looked down. It read twelve hours, twenty-nine minutes. It was counting down. Twelve hours and twenty-nine—no, now make that twenty-eight—minutes to save the world. Juni took a big, deep breath. The doors opened, and the bright white light blinded him until an agent slipped a pair of sunglasses on him.

"Wear these glasses," said Donnagon. "Keep them on throughout the entire game. You're being sent into a zero-gravity chamber alongside Carmen. It will give you a competitive edge. When you're in there, things will feel real to you."

"Are they real?" Juni wanted to know.

Donnagon stepped back, not saying a word.

Juni looked in front of him. A man checked his stopwatch, and pointed to a man on his right. He checked his watch, then pointed to a man near Juni. This guy pointed right at Juni and . . . *BLAST!* Juni shot forward though a tunnel.

"Remember!" shouted Donnagon. "Find Carmen! Shut down the game . . . and don't let the Toymaker out!"

CHAPTER 5

THUMP! Juni landed—hard—on the floor. He tapped it. It was hollow.

"Computer generated," Juni said. He stood and looked around. He was in a garishly colored, chaotic world. Kids and toads on pogo sticks pounded the ground like jackhammers as they went by. Kids, who had to be beta testers, scrambled into battle, screaming out orders to each other. One pogo bouncer, a tall, spiky-haired boy, bounced way higher than the others. He leaped as high as a building, screaming orders to his foot soldiers.

Just then Juni spotted a mysterious girl watching him from an alleyway. He ran over to her, but she disappeared. He looked back down the street. One of the beta testers dragged a large burlap sack behind him. He was collecting gold coins and he looked tired, unable to keep up with the rest of the beta testers.

"Catch up, Arnold!" another beta tester called out.

"I need more points, Rez!" shouted Arnold.

"Earn their trust," Juni said softly to himself. "And they'll help me."

Juni started to follow Arnold, but a group of menacing toads got in his way. Juni watched, openmouthed, as Arnold unleashed a flurry of skull-crushing roundhouse kicks and brutally fast punches, knocking the toads down. They quickly hopped away. As Arnold picked up a fallen gold coin and examined it, he spotted Juni. Juni, remembering the skull-crushing kicks, backed up nervously. Arnold came closer and closer, dragging the burlap bag. Juni backed up farther, against a wall. Arnold reached forward and pushed Juni out of the way, then reached down and picked up a gold coin that Juni had been standing on. He tossed it into his bag, then leaped on a pogo stick being ridden by a toad. Arnold claimed the pogo stick as his own by swinging the heavy bag of coins at the amphibian, sending it flying.

Juni considered the situation. While knocking toads senseless didn't look particularly easy, it did look doable. When the next pogo stick approached, Juni readied himself. When it got close, Juni ran and jumped on it. Assuming it was manned by another toad, he prepared to shove the rider off.

"Get your own ride, creepo!" a voice yelled. Juni looked and realized it was another player.

"Sorry," Juni said, "I thought you were a toad."

"New player, huh?" the kid said.

"Yeah," Juni admitted.

"Here's a quick lesson you won't soon forget," said the kid, whose name was Francis.

Francis's shoulder plate opened and an apparatus shot out, whacking Juni off the pogo stick. Juni fell off a bridge, three stories down, down, down. *BOOM!* He hit the ground. Hard.

He groaned. This was *not* going to be easy.

◎ ◎ ◎

Meanwhile, back at OSS headquarters, Cesca entered the main room.

"How is he?" she demanded.

"Brain waves normal," confirmed Donnagon.

"But how *is* he?" Cesca prodded.

"Oh," said Donnagon. "He fell."

CHAPTER 6

Back in the game, Juni was lying flat on the ground.

"Stand up," a computerized voice commanded. Juni looked up to find that he was being scanned by a floating robot head. It was Orbit, the game Advice Counselor.

"What happened?" Juni asked groggily.

"You fell three stories," Orbit explained.

"I survived?" Juni said hopefully.

"Not exactly," Orbit said gravely.

Juni watched as a counter clicked from "ten" to "nine."

"That is your life counter," Orbit explained. "After taking heavy damage you lose a life."

Juni didn't want to ask, but he had to. "What happens when it hits zero?"

"Game Over," said Orbit.

"Do I start over?" Juni asked hopefully.

"When you run out of life, you lose. No replays. No restarts," Orbit explained solemnly.

"Tough game," said Juni. What an understatement!

"The toughest there is," Orbit admitted. "Better hurry!"

Juni checked his watch. He shook his wrist. Something must have happened in the fall, because his countdown watch was definitely broken.

"What happed to my twelve hours?" he shouted. "I only have four now!"

"Time flies when you're playing games," explained Orbit, flying away, raining ooze as he went.

"This is crazy," said Juni, swatting away the ooze.

The ooze got bigger. Juni stepped on it, looked around, and then stepped up to the next one. Floating ooze stairs! Cool!

Orbit floated by. "Use your belt," he said.

Juni shrugged and hit his belt. Jets popped out of his shoes.

"Thanks," said Juni. "But how do I get to . . ."

Orbit interrupted. "If the programmerz find out I'm even helping you this much, I'll be erased from the game's hard drive. Good luck."

Juni climbed back to the bridge he had fallen from and came face-to-face with Francis, the guy who had knocked him off the pogo stick.

"Who are you?' asked Francis, his eyes narrowed.

"I'm Juni Cortez, ex–secret agent of the OSS. I need to get to Level Five," Juni explained in a rush. "I only have a few hours. . . ."

Arnold suddenly appeared next to Juni. "Level Five is unwinnable," he said knowingly.

"I understand that," said Juni.

"Rez!" called Francis. "This person thinks he's Level Five material."

"So I hear," said Rez, coming·over.

Juni checked his notes. "You must be a beta tester," he said.

Rez nodded. "One of the first allowed to roam free in these coveted digital hills, my friend. How can I offer service? I'm Rez."

"Hi, Rez," said Juni. Finally, he was getting somewhere! "Get me cheat codes to Level Five. Back door entrance, short cuts. Anything. I can pay you with bonus packs." He flashed some illegal packets the agents had given him.

The three examined the packs suspiciously.

"I can see I'm earning your trust," Juni joked.

Rez looked up. "No cheat codes are allowed in this game, my friend. Implementation of any form of hack code or cheat boost will trigger an immediate Game Over and a permanent evac from the game."

"It's all in your tech manual," added Francis.

As Juni watched in disbelief, Arnold took the bonus packs from Juni and crushed them with his bare hands. "You have to play by the rules," he said solemnly. "Or not at all!"

Juni checked his watch. Time was running out! "All right, then how do I get to Level Two as quickly as possible? Lives are at stake. Please."

Rez pointed. "See that target? Hit it. You'll bounce straight to the moon."

Juni stared. "I hit that, and I'll bounce to the moon?" he asked skeptically.

"Well, you have to hit it pretty hard," Rez said.

Francis nodded. "I suggest a running start. Level Two is on the dark side of the moon. Only way to get there is by hitting that target and bouncing to it."

"Not a lot of realism going on in these games, is there?" said Juni. He took a deep breath, ran to the target, and jumped on it. He bounced up high and hard.

"Where did you just send him?" Arnold asked.

"To the Arena of Misfortune," Rez replied breezily. "Won't be seeing him anymore!"

"The less competition, the better," Francis said to the others.

CHAPTER 7

Juni had hit the target on its sweet spot, and he was *still* flying

"Fly me to the moon, huh?" Juni said. "So much for making friends." He flew up, up, and then suddenly started to fall down. Hard. And fast.

Juni grimaced. "This is gonna hurt," he predicted.

Juni fell straight down onto another target, again hitting it dead center. He bounced, picking up speed. There was one more huge target left, just over a high hill. Just as Juni hit it, a creature closed its huge mouth over the target. Juni screamed, bounced, and began to flail his arms and legs so he would fly faster through the air and out of reach of the creature's snapping jaws. Juni just barely managed to avoid the creature's teeth before he flew into space.

He watched the earth get smaller and smaller beneath him. Despite the bizarre situation he was in, Juni still managed to appreciate the beauty. "Wow. That is truly spectacular," he commented. As the earth got smaller, the moon grew larger and larger. Finally, Juni landed hard on its dusty gray surface, then skidded across it until he came to a stop. He spit out a mouthful of moon dust, then, though he was quite groggy, managed to stand. He looked down at the earth, sparkling below like a shiny blue pearl.

CLICK! Another life gone. He was down to eight.

"Oh, great!" Juni groaned.

Orbit appeared and buzzed around Juni's head.

"A message from OSS," he announced. "Do you accept?"

"Please," said Juni.

Orbit produced a holographic screen. The faces of the Agents Giggles appeared. "Okay, Juni," said Donnagon. "After Level One we can no longer be of assistance."

Assistance? "What assistance . . ." Juni began.

Donnagon broke in. "It's all up to you from here on out," he explained.

"However," Cesca added, "you do get one additional lifeline, which you can choose to use now or later."

A lifeline! No time like the present! *"Now!"* Juni cried. "Give it to me *now*!"

"You can bring in any one person from the outside to help you on your journey," Cesca explained.

"I can bring one person into the game?" Juni asked.

"Correct," replied Donnagon.

"Call up the family files," Juni commanded.

Now the screens filled with a whole new set of faces.

"Mom's stats, please," said Juni.

Orbit began to read: "Pros: Assertive. Athletic. Strategist. Knows karate."

"Good, good," said Juni. "Yeah, that's all very . . ."

"Cons," continued Orbit.

Juni's mouth fell open. "Cons? What cons? Mom has no cons!"

"Forgetful. Distracted. Can overthink a situation. Easily fooled," said Orbit.

"Now, that's not very fair," said Juni.

"Mom is ruled out," pronounced Orbit.

"No!" cried Juni. "Don't rule her out yet. I just want to see some other choices before I make up my mind."

Gregorio popped onscreen.

"Pros," read Orbit. "Intelligent. Resourceful. Methodical. Reliable. Stealth specialist."

The cons list appeared for Gregorio next. Juni's eyes bugged out of his head. It looked like it was a mile long!

"Cons," Orbit began. "Unreliable. Forgetful. Nervous. May crack under pressure. Worrywart."

"Dad does worry a lot," recalled Juni. "Ugh. Okay. Next."

Valentin's picture came up next. Automatically, Juni reached up and touched his necklace.

Orbit began to speak. "Pros: Bold. Resourceful. Superior intellect. Master chess player. Mysterious. Cons: Physically disabled."

Juni noticed that Grandpa's energy was not graphed in from the waist down. Interesting.

"Moving on," said Orbit.

Uncle Machete's picture appeared.

Juni had an idea. "Wait a minute. Go back to Grandpa," he said. He studied Valentin's photo. "Physically disabled," he mused. "Hmmmmm . . ."

"What are you thinking, sir?" Orbit asked.

"He's been paralyzed from the waist down for thirty years. Where did the energy force get transferred to?" Juni thought for a moment. "It had to go somewhere."

Orbit displayed Valentin's body graph. The energy in his head and upper body surged with a red glow.

Juni nodded. "It would have doubled back

again, making his arms, his heart, his *brain*, twice as strong as a normal person."

Juni grinned. "No wonder he always beat me at canasta! I choose Grandpa!"

"Selected," said the robot.

Juni breathed a sigh of relief. Grandpa was coming. Everything was going to be all right.

CHAPTER 8

The game suddenly split open, and Valentin wheeled himself out.

"That was fast!" said Juni, surprised.

Valentin looked around, confused. "Juni? Where . . . where am I?"

"The moon, Grandpa," Juni explained. "In a game. Run by a madman called the Toymaker. Long story."

"The Toymaker is here?" Valentin asked in disbelief.

"You know him?" said Juni.

"I've been hunting him down," Valentin revealed, "for almost thirty years."

He looked right into Juni's eyes. "You should not have brought me here, Juni."

Juni's heart sank. "I needed your help," he explained. "We have to find Carmen and shut down the game. It goes online in . . ." He checked his watch. ". . . three hours and will cause great harm to the world if . . ."

"What is that?" Valentin said, interrupting.

Above their heads floated a power-up.

"A power-up of some kind," said Juni, reaching up for it and reading the inscription. "Mega Legs."

"Give it to me," Valentin said urgently.

Juni tossed it to his grandfather. As soon as Valentin caught it, he began glowing. Juni had to shield his eyes from the blindingly bright glow. And all of a sudden, to Juni's amazement, Valentin was standing!

"Grandpa!" Juni sputtered. "Your legs! You can really . . . walk!"

Valentin shook his head. "No, Juni . . ." He bent his legs and sprang into the air, flipping over Juni's head and making a perfect landing. "I can do more than that," he said, a merry gleam in his eye. He spoke softly to himself. "Once a dream, now a reality." A butterfly fluttered by his head. "More wonderful than I ever imagined." He started chasing the butterfly, doing flips and somersaults after it.

"Grandpa, where are you going?" Juni shouted worriedly.

"Don't wait for me, Juni, I'll catch up with you!" Valentin called back, still in hot pursuit of the butterfly.

"But we have to find Carmen!" Juni yelled.

Valentin didn't hear him. He was long gone, hopping and skipping and chasing butterflies, using the legs that he hadn't been able to use for the past thirty years.

◎ ◎ ◎

Meanwhile, deep in his brainlike chamber, the Toymaker twisted a key into the side of an old metal bird toy. It fluttered its little metal wings.

"Valentin. My old friend," the Toymaker said. "You think you will catch me this time, don't you? Well . . . surprise . . . you will!" He put the bird down and picked up a holographic image of Valentin happily chasing after the butterfly.

"Everything falls into place," the Toymaker said solemnly. He turned and faced the glowing orb in the center of the room.

"Everything . . . falls," the Toymaker repeated.

Inside the orb Carmen slept, rotating slowly.

CHAPTER 9

Juni entered the Arena of Misfortune. It was a large arena that had robots for pillars. Giant chunks of metal flew out of the walls and smacked to the ground around him.

Cheers were heard from within. Juni stepped through the entrance and took a look around. The huge arena was jam-packed with spectators. Computer-generated ones, and not very good ones at that. They cheered as Juni entered.

"A courageous new contestant!" a voice shouted. Juni took a look. It was a boy. He looked again. Correction. Make that a boy with oddly long fingers. "Welcome to the Robocon," Long-Fingered Boy said.

"I need to get to Level Two," Juni said.

"Well, you came to the wrong place. This is the Arena of Misfortune. If you want to get to Level

Two from here, you have to go to Battle-a Mech."
He led Juni to an elevator platform. Juni began to
rise to the top.

"How do I do that?" Juni called.

"I'll explain it to you up there," said Long-
Fingered Boy.

The substandard CG spectators cheered and
shouted. Juni got to the top, and there stood Long-
Fingered Boy. Juni blinked. How did *that* happen?

"Just go out there in your robot chassis—and
FIGHT!" he shouted, shoving Juni into a Robotic
chair. A chest plate and attachments slammed
down, locking him in. Juni struggled against
them. "Wait a minute, who am I fighting?" he
called.

"Her," said Long-Fingered Boy, pointing to a
red-haired girl being strapped into her Mech. It
was the girl who had been watching Juni when he
first arrived in the game. Her name was Demetra.
And, boy, did she look tough.

A giant wall split into two, opening to reveal
that Juni and his chassis were actually the head of
a robot. He looked down. A *giant* robot.

Across the way, Demetra, also part of a huge
robot, strode out of her corral.

Long-Fingered Boy paused to give one more
piece of advice. "Oh, um, don't get too trashed and
I win bonus points," he said.

It was time for action. Juni tried to make his robot step forward, but only managed to stumble out into the middle of the arena. Smooth move, he said to himself. Then it all began to make sense. Juni moved his foot, and the robot moved his foot. When Juni moved his arm, the robot moved his arm. Juni began to get the hang of it and managed to step into the arena, right in front of Demetra.

As a floating ref explained the rules, Juni took a closer look at his opponent. She looked very tough, very pretty, and very serious.

Juni decided it was time for introductions. "Hi, I'm Juni," he said, extending his arm for a handshake. Big mistake! The huge robotic arm also extended and smacked Demetra's robot in the head. *Oops!*

Demetra narrowed her eyes and hit Juni's robot with a roundhouse punch. *WHAM!* Demetra waved at Juni. "Hi, I'm Demetra," she said.

Juni stumbled back and hit the ground—hard. The CG crowd roared its approval.

Juni shook it off and got back up. So did the robot.

The battle began. Punches, kicks, elbows, and knees were thrown. Juni kept checking his life meter—he was losing lives, and quick. Must win for Carmen, he thought to himself. And suddenly,

38

amazingly, he *was* winning, using his smarts instead of his robotic brawn. Victory!

Long-Fingered Boy strode over. "Well, well, well," he said. "For a kid who doesn't know how to fight, you sure know how to fight. Congratulations. And ah . . . keep the suit."

He reached one of his long fingers toward Juni.

"What are you doing?' demanded Juni.

The long metal finger reached out and hit the EJECT button. *SPRONG!* Juni was ejected from the hot seat and flew out of the arena.

"Good luck, kid," said Long-Fingered Boy, watching him. "You'll need it where you're going. Level Two . . . here you gooooo. . . ."

CHAPTER 10

*B*OOM! Juni crash landed somewhere in Level Two, smack down on his life counter. *Click.* Another life gone.

"Uggghhhh," Juni groaned. He rose shakily to his feet and began to explore Level Two.

◎ ◎ ◎

The Toymaker paced the brainlike room, surrounded by his advisors.

"Let's go over this again, shall we?" said the Toymaker. "So we make no mistakes. So there are no gross errors. So there is no lack of communication among us."

The advisors were silent.

"What I want," continued the Toymaker. "What *we* want . . ." He paused. "What do we want?" he asked the group.

"Our time on this planet is over. It belongs now to our youth," said one advisor, who was very clever.

"But only if we rule their minds!" shouted another advisor, who, truth be told, was a bit of a dictator.

"We could start the world over," chimed in another advisor. "Cure it of its disease. We could begin anew." He was the good one.

The Toymaker tossed his little metal windup bird at the Good Advisor. It sailed right through him. The other advisors looked at each other, puzzled.

"Forget what we *can* do," thundered the Toymaker. "Is there something we *should* do? Am I doing the right thing?"

The Toymaker stared at his advisors—who were actually mirror images of himself. Each advisor represented a different side of the Toymaker's personality.

The Clever Advisor thought for a moment. Then he spoke. "It is not about doing the right thing, it's about doing the smart thing. We won't be able to escape from here otherwise."

The Dictator Advisor was in full agreement. "I speak for all of us when I say, 'We want out!'" he said. "The end justifies the means."

"You have their attention," said the Good Advisor. Then he paused for a moment. "The question is, What are you teaching them?"

"The time for takeover is NOW!" shouted the Dictatorial Advisor.

The Toymaker looked very confused. There were too many opinions. Questioning all the advice, he looked at the advisors before him. "Who are you people?"

The advisors spoke in unison. "I am you!"

"Forgive me," responded the Toymaker. "I forget the extent of my programming powers from time to time. For a moment . . . for a moment" —he laughed sheepishly—". . . I believed you all actually existed!"

The Toymaker hit a button marked ME. The advisors disappeared, and the Toymaker turned back to his game.

"The great game of life is over, my friends," he said. "But a *new* game is about to begin." He watched a hologram of Juni as he walked away from the arena.

◎ ◎ ◎

Mounted over the arena was a large GAME OVER billboard. On it was a mysterious figure in a sharp-looking suit. Juni stood in front of the figure, not realizing that he was a dead ringer for—The Guy.

Francis, Rez, and Arnold stepped forward. They stared in disbelief.

"Hold on to your joysticks," Rez pronounced. "I think we got him."

Juni saw the three and stepped toward them.

Arnold stared. "You're The Guy," he said in awe.

"I'm the *who*?" asked Juni, confused.

"The Guy!" said Francis. "The Guy from the poster." He pointed to the billboard behind Juni. "*That* guy."

Juni turned around. Francis was right. Weird. But no biggie. Juni had more important things to worry about.

"I'm just looking for my sister," Juni explained. "She's somewhere on Level Four, and then we're heading out through Level Five."

"To win the game?" Arnold asked in disbelief.

How much to tell? Juni took the safe route. "I guess . . . that's one way of putting it," he said.

"'Cause, see," said Francis, "the tech manual states that if we find The Guy"—he pointed to the Juni-ish poster guy—"he'll lead us through the unwinnable level."

"Just 'cause he makes it out of the Robocon in one piece doesn't mean he's The Guy," Rez argued.

Francis would not be discouraged. "He's the first I've seen make it out of there in a power suit."

"Give me a break," scoffed Rez. "This wimp's a phony."

Francis shrugged. "There's only one way to find out."

Behind them was a huge spooky-looking race-track. It seemed to extend forever.

"Mega Race!" said Rez.

Francis stared at Juni levelly. "Only The Guy could win Mega Race."

"But I'm not The Guy," Juni protested. "I already told you."

Juni jumped as an unseen announcer's voice boomed: *"THE RACE WILL BEGIN SHORTLY. CLAIM YOUR VEHICLE."*

Arnold shoved Juni. Hard. "Let's go," he said.

Against his better judgment, Juni began making his way to the track.

When he arrived, Juni spotted a mysterious stranger staring at him. He ignored it and climbed into the car. It was a tiny bumper car, and Juni's head poked out of the top like a giant balloon.

"You've got to be kidding," he said.

The cars moved forward, connecting to bigger vehicles. Juni ended up in the tank.

"All right!" he shouted. Not bad! Things were improving.

Rez pulled up next to Juni on a Sonic Cycle. Francis was nearby.

"The race will tell us if you're The Guy," said Francis. "If you are, you can hang with us. If you're a phony . . ."

". . . I will crush you," finished Arnold, who had just pulled up beside Juni.

"But I'm not The Guy," Juni explained for what felt like the millionth time. "How many times do I have to say it?"

The announcer's voice boomed: *"THERE IS ONE GAME RULE IN THIS RACE,"* it said. *"WIN AT ANY COST."*

"We'll try to help you," said Rez. "As much as we can. . . ."

"THE RACE WILL BEGIN NOW!"

Juni gulped.

CHAPTER 11

The track was insane. The cars were going faster than seemed humanly possible. And the twists and turns of the track weren't the only danger in store. Juni was under attack! A rider on an electrified chariot turned and aimed a lightning bolt baton at Juni, electrifying his vehicle.

Hmm, did *he* have any powers? Juni looked down and saw several buttons on the console. A banana. An apple. A pineapple. Juni liked apples. He pushed the button. *SPRONG!* A giant apple pie was launched from his vehicle. It flipped through the air, landing on Lightning Bolt Guy and completely wiping him out. The smashed pie on the track created an unbelievable slick that caused several of Juni's competitors to spin out of control and crash. *BOOM! BOOM! BOOM!*

"Easy as pie," Juni said with a chuckle.

Oh no! Lightning Bolt Guy was back. And he didn't look very happy with Juni. Rez rode up alongside him.

"Juni! Push the red button!" he yelled.

"Why?" said Juni.

"PUSH IT!" Rez insisted. "It's the only thing that will work!"

"Are you sure?" asked Juni. Should he trust this Rez character? Was this guy trying to trick him?

"Yes!" Rez shouted.

Juni located the red button. He hesitated. For on it in big bold letters was the warning: DO NOT PUSH.

Behind Juni's back, Rez smiled wickedly and backed off.

Juni took a deep breath and pushed the button. Uh-oh. The whole vehicle locked up and began to flip. Juni leaped on top of it, running along it as it spun, like a logroller. He leaped off, landed on the track, and grabbed the tail end of Rez's bike. *Ooof!* Rez kept going, and Juni was dragged along behind. Sparks were flying and Juni was getting some extreme road rash.

"Rez!" Juni shouted. "Give me a hand!"

"I can't!" replied Rez. "How about a foot?"

"Okay," said Juni, relieved.

Rez turned and stomped on Juni's fingers with his boot. *Yeow!* Juni was forced to let go.

"You asked for it, Guy!" crowed Rez. "Ha-ha-ha-ha-ha-ha!" He turned around just in time to see Juni's abandoned tank stopped in the middle of the track. There was no time to swerve. Rez hit the tank full speed and flipped end over end until he had completely cleared the track, landing on another vehicle.

"After him!" Rez shouted. He was furious. "That way! Move!"

Juni, still skidding backward on the ground, just managed to roll out of the way of an oncoming vehicle. He passed Arnold's Big Wheel bike.

"Give me your hand, Juni!" shouted Arnold.

But Juni didn't know who to trust anymore. He let Arnold pass him by. Arnold was crushed. He really did want to help.

Juni was still sliding, eating dust the whole way. Finally, a strange vehicle pulled up beside him. A hand reached down, grabbed his collar, and lifted him. Juni looked up gratefully. It was his grandfather—driving a really cool Mega Racer.

"You're supposed to be winning this race, Juni!" Valentin scolded.

"Where did you go?" asked Juni.

"Look what I caught!" Valentin responded. He opened his hand to reveal the beautiful butterfly he had been chasing earlier. It flew away.

"Oh, I'll have to get that," said Valentin,

watching it go. Then he turned back to Juni. "First, let's get you back in the race," he said, putting the pedal to the metal. They blasted forward, Juni dangling off the side.

Valentin raced up to another driver, placing Juni on the back on his vehicle. He reached over, plucked the driver off, and backed up. Quickly, Juni grabbed the bike's controls and zoomed forward.

"Pardon me, but does your suit come equipped with a parachute?" Valentin asked the driver.

"Yeah, why?" the driver answered, confused.

"Ah, good," Valentin said helpfully, right before he dropped him over the side of the track. The driver's parachute opened and he floated away.

Juni was now on a single track, and all the racers were about to converge. They were neck to neck, when the track took a sharp turn upward.

"What is this . . . ?" Juni said in disbelief.

At the top of the rise all the racers began to free-fall, because the track just simply—ended. Nothing more. End of the line. The racers all hurtled into the air and landed on the other side of the track. When Rez landed, he knocked the other driver off the vehicle he had commandeered.

"My turn, sucker," he said. Next, he reached into his bike and pulled out an enormous boxing glove. He aimed it right at Juni, almost hitting him square in the jaw.

Arnold sped up to Juni. "The glove! Grab the glove!" he shouted.

Juni reached out, plucked the glove from Rez, and fastened it to his bike.

However, the glove was still attached to Rez's bike. Juni sped up, dragging Rez along. Juni then hit the scissors button on his vehicle, and a huge pair of scissors popped out and snipped the glove holder. Rez flew back, hitting a few other racers in the process. But not Valentin. He dodged out of the way, popped a wheelie, and shot off. Juni wondered if his grandfather was off butterfly-hunting again. Hopefully not.

Rex regained control of his gloveless vehicle and chased after Arnold.

"What are you doing?" Rez demanded.

"Helping The Guy," Arnold explained.

Rez couldn't believe what he was hearing. "You can't help him yet. We're not sure if it's really him!"

"I'm sure," Arnold said simply.

Furious, Rez reached over and pushed the parachute button on Arnold's bike. Arnold watched as a parachute flew out. The parachute strings unraveled and unraveled and unraveled . . .

"I will crush you," said Arnold softly.

. . . until a tiny parachute popped out. It was just big enough to snap Arnold back with great force. Arnold's gold coins went flying everywhere.

"Not today, Muscles," scoffed Rez. "Haaaaa!" And then a moment later: "Argh!" He and all the riders had just flown off the track and began to free-fall down into the tunnels deep below.

Juni picked what looked like a cool tunnel, landed, and began to pick up speed. It looked like he was way ahead of everyone else. But not for long.

The track ended, leaving nothing but a sharp fall. Juni slammed on his brakes and skidded to the edge.

The other racers were hot on his heels. They slammed right into the back of his vehicle and everyone plummeted. Juni's life counter clicked. One more gone!

Just as Juni was about to hit the ground, Valentin flew by with some advice. "Grab another bike, Juni!" he called. Juni reached out, grabbed a bike, and climbed aboard. The rest of the racers followed suit. Everyone landed—*CRASH!*—and the race continued! Faster than ever!

Suddenly, a bolt machine pulled up beside Juni. Rez was riding it and began hurling bolt sticks at him. Juni managed to dodge them and they hit Arnold instead, who skidded right onto another track. Arnold's electrified vehicle slammed into Rez's, and they both went spinning wildly out of control, past Juni. "Wow," said Juni.

"Final stretch," the announcer announced. Just then a mysterious rider in a Big Clamp vehicle began pinching Juni's car with its monstrous clamp, tearing off the back of his vehicle. After a moment of confusion, Juni improvised by jumping feet first onto the seat and riding it that way.

The stranger next loaded a spike sphere and blasted it right at Juni, taking away the body of Juni's bike completely.

Here goes nothing, thought Juni, doing a handstand on what remained of the bike.

But that wasn't all. The Big Clamp vehicle also sported a cannon, loaded with a bunch of smaller spike spheres. They were all launched at Juni.

"TEN SECONDS TO END OF RACE," said the announcer.

BOOM! The spheres took out the top of Juni's bike. He was now standing on the wheel bolts, riding it like a unicycle!

"EIGHT SECONDS!" the announcer's voice boomed.

"Six, five, four . . ." the announcer counted down.

The stranger fired more spheres at Juni. The entire tire exploded, leaving only—the hubcap. Miraculously, Juni landed directly inside it, and began to skid across the track. The track suddenly split into rails, and Juni rode the sliding hubcap along the middle one. The Big Clamp tried to follow, but tipped sideways, getting stuck.

"Three, two, one," said the announcer.

Juni hubcapped it across the finish line, the other racers right behind him.

"WINNER BY A HUBCAP . . . JUNI CORTEZ!"

CHAPTER 12

The other racers skid to a massive simultaneous stop. They dismounted their vehicles and looked up in awe at Juni. He rose from his "vehicle" slowly, and stepped to the side, placing his foot on the hubcap and flipping it deftly into his hand. He walked forward silently. Confidently. After all, he was The Guy.

"I thought you were him," said Francis in awe.

"I *knew* it," Arnold clarified.

Even Rez stepped forward. "I guess you are," he admitted.

Just then Juni spotted the mysterious stranger dismounting the Big Clamp vehicle. Someone ran up and whispered in the stranger's ear, all the while pointing at Juni.

The mysterious stranger approached Juni and removed his—make that, her—helmet. It was Demetra, the girl from the Arena of Misfortune.

Coolly, she looked Juni up and down. "So, I hear you're The Guy," she said.

Everyone watched Juni, holding their breath. What would he say?

Juni started to shake his head, but then corrected himself. "I am . . . definitely The Guy," he heard himself saying.

All the racers burst into cheers and began clapping Juni on the back. Demetra actually smiled.

Valentin pulled in on his Mega Racer.

"So, now what, Guy?" Rez asked.

"Hold on," said Juni. "I have to talk to my grandfather."

"To who?" Rez asked, confused.

Juni quickly corrected himself. "I mean . . . I must confer with The Wizard of Atari-Sega-Nendo!"

Rez nodded. That sounded better. "Yeah, okay, cool."

Valentin was playing with the butterfly he had just recaught. "Congratulations, you won the race," he commented.

"But now they think I'm some important guy who's going to win the game for them," Juni explained. He thought for a moment. "Is that good or bad?"

Valentin considered the question. "For our purposes," he said, "that is very good. They can lead us to Level Four more quickly. So we can find your sister, so we can shut down the game, make things right . . ."

Valentin got out of his vehicle. Juni did a double take. He had no idea his grandfather was so tall! He looked so strong and powerful—almost like a gray-haired superhero!

". . . and so I can find the Toymaker," Valentin finished. He leaned in closer to his grandson. "But they have to believe you are someone important. And in order for them to believe, *you* must believe, Juni."

"We're not supposed to get near the Toymaker," Juni reminded him.

"So say the rules of the OSS, which I am not following," Valentin said pointedly.

What was his grandfather saying?

"But . . . he might escape. We can't risk that!" Juni began.

"Guy!" Rez called impatiently.

"We'll talk about this later," Juni said sternly. He walked back to the group to fill them in.

"Okay, here it is—I'm not supposed to lead you to Level Five," Juni explained.

"You're not?" said Rez. He looked confused.

"You're supposed to lead me there," said Juni.

"When we get there, I get you through the unwinnable level."

Everyone looked at each other.

"You mean we all work together?" Francis asked.

"The Wizard says that if we work together we all win," Juni responded.

"With my strength," Arnold said.

"My brains," Francis added.

"My cool," Rez stated.

Demetra stepped forward. "And my . . . intuition."

"Okay, good," said Rez. "So you're The Guy, and we're counting on you."

Juni nodded.

"But," Rez continued, pointing to Juni's counter, "if you fail us or you're not who you say you are, this life counter will hit zero faster than you can say oops."

Juni gulped. Point taken. "Deal," he said. "First I gotta pick someone up. So . . . Level Three, people, right now. Move."

Juni checked his watch and his eyes nearly bugged out of his head. Two hours remaining! He crossed his fingers at Valentin for luck. Valentin gave Juni a mysterious look. He was still playing with the butterfly.

◎ ◎ ◎

Back at OSS headquarters, Donnagon and Cesca

were keeping score of the competitive game.

"He's doing good, eh?" said Cesca.

"He's doing great," Donnagon admitted. "And that's the problem."

Cesca looked at him quizzically. "Why?"

"They must have called too much attention to themselves," Donnagon explained, checking the readouts. "They've awoken the programmerz."

"The programmerz!" Cesca cried in dismay. "Pull him out of there!"

"Too late," Donnagon said sadly.

◎ ◎ ◎

Valentin, Juni, and the kids . . . make that The Wizard, The Guy, and the kids walked into a vast empty space made entirely of metal. One of the kids jumped as a giant bolt of lightning crashed across the sky.

"I know this is just a game, but I'm scared," Francis admitted.

"Don't wet your pants," scoffed Demetra. "You might get us all electrocuted."

Rez snickered.

"How about I hold on to you?" Francis suggested.

Demetra looked panicked. "Don't touch me!" she said.

As the group made their way deeper into the

Juni and Carmen are geared up to take on the Toymaker! These spies won't let a little thing like a mind-twisting virtual-reality video game stop them from beating their newest enemy at his own game.

The Toymaker is a man out for some serious revenge.
His plan? Use an evil video game to control the minds
of children everywhere.

Carmen Cortez is the top OSS computer hacker. She skillfully injects a computer virus into the mainframe of GAME OVER. But she gets caught in the game.

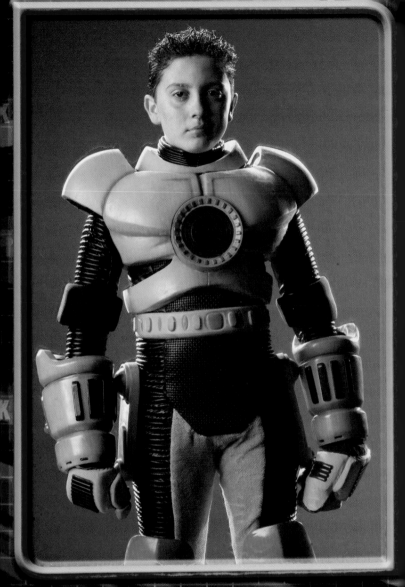

Now that Carmen is trapped inside the Toymaker's game, it is up to Juni to rescue her before it is too late!

The beta testers—Francis, Rez, and Arnold are some expert gamers who want to win—without losing lives!

Demetra and the other beta testers know their way around the levels, but will they help Juni rescue Carmen and take on the Toymaker?

Juni has a soft spot for the clever Demetra—even though she's betrayed him.

The programmerz are the dudes who wrote the security codes and guard the game. They have only one mission—stop the gamers from getting to the next level.

Carmen and Juni know that it takes more than just skill to beat the bad guys—it takes trust and teamwork! With this team working together, the Toymaker is going to lose.

vast space, things began to pop out at them. Everyone stepped forward to protect The Guy.

"All right, this is cool," said Juni reassuringly. "We'll get there in no time."

Suddenly loud noises erupted all around them. Whistles and buzzing sounds echoed off the metal walls. Scanners popped up everywhere the eye could see.

"Uh-oh," said Francis.

"Uh-oh what?" asked Juni.

"Programmerz," said Rex. "They're on to us. But why?"

"What *are* the programmerz, again?" asked Valentin.

"The brainiacs that wrote the book of the game," Francis explained.

"So they work for the Toymaker?" Valentin asked.

"Programmerz are the reason you found us on Level One," put in Rez. "They caught Francis cheating during the Mega Race. They'll bounce us back to Level One again if they catch us."

Juni checked his watch. "I don't have time for that!" he cried.

"Spread out!" Arnold commanded. Everyone scattered. Juni looked around wildly. What happened to everyone working together?

"Don't split up!" Juni shouted. "That never works! If we just stick together. . . ."

Juni felt defeated. This was all wrong. Then he brightened. At least he had *one* person to stand by him. "Okay, Grandpa, I guess it's you and . . ." He looked around, but no one was there. ". . . me. Hello? . . . Grandpa?"

CHAPTER 13

Juni looked around apprehensively. The whistling sounds kept echoing around him and he saw some spooky-looking shadowy shapes rising over a nearby hill. Not good. Juni began to run.

"Psst!" someone hissed.

Ahhh! What was that? Juni nearly jumped out of his skin. Then he looked and saw it was Demetra, waving him over. He ran over to join her.

She rolled her eyes. "Can't you at least try and *act* like you're The Guy?" she asked.

What? Was his cover blown? "You . . . you know my secret?" he whispered.

Demetra leaned forward. "I've seen The Guy," she said, "and you're not him."

Well, the jig was up. Juni changed the subject. "Why are the programmerz chasing us?" he asked.

"Someone has a game cheat," said Demetra, handing Juni a map.

"What's this?" he asked.

"A map to the game," Demetra said.

Juni was shocked. "This is illegal!" he said.

"You want to find your sister or not?" Demetra asked, glancing up at the programmerz. Now that they were closer, Juni could take a better look. He stared. They were beatnik-looking guys, with knit caps and goatees. They snapped their fingers and danced through the streets on their search. Juni shook his head. This place was getting more bizarre by the minute!

"We just need *them* to believe you're The Guy and we'll get out of here," Demetra said.

Juni blinked. That was so familiar! "That's exactly what The Wizard said," said Juni.

"Who, your grandpa?" Demetra asked.

Man, she was good! "You just know all my secrets now," said Juni.

"Don't worry," said Demetra. "Your secret's safe with me."

Juni stared at Demetra in awe. How cool was *she*?

"Let's go this way," Demetra suggested. "I have a plan."

Juni followed, no questions asked.

◉ ◉ ◉

The programmerz continued to circle, looking for them. Cool! thought Juni, they're falling right into our trap! They spotted Demetra and began to tail her, bumping right into Juni. "Grandpa! Help!" Juni cried.

"Oh, listen to that, E Dog," said a programmer named Logos, his voice dripping with sarcasm. "He's calling his grandpa. I'm so scared."

"Come and get me, Gramps," scoffed E dog, with a laugh. "What's he gonna do, drool on us?"

Just then Valentin grabbed their collars and lifted them up. *Way* up.

"Why are you picking on my grandson?" he asked.

The programmerz just stared back mutely, their eyes glazed over with fear.

"Why?" Valentin asked again.

The other kids all ran forward. "That's Logos and E Dog, the leaders!" Francis exclaimed.

Valentin looked at them more closely. "You're programmerz? Nice outfits—let's see what you really look like, eh?" He pulled one of their scanners away from them and began scanning them. Suddenly, their true selves appeared. The supercool beatniks were revealed to be loser computer geeks.

"Computer nerds!" crowed Rez.

"Very unimpressive," said Valentin, shaking his

head. "Now tell me, where is the Toymaker? Where?"

Juni started getting nervous. What was his grandfather up to? "Grandpa—uh—Wizard? Put them down!" he shouted.

"After I teach them a lesson," said Valentin.

"It's been taught," Juni said. "Drop 'em."

Valentin looked at Juni. Seeing how serious he was, he set the two programmerz down. They ran away like the wind.

"You were going to hurt them?" asked Juni.

"Not at all," Valentin said with a wink. "But look at how fast they're running. It's absolutely amazing."

Valentin laughed as Juni threw his arms around him.

Valentin looked over at Demetra and his smile faded. Demetra shook her head.

"Let's move on, shall we?" Valentin said, his face now serious.

"Yes, we should move on," Demetra agreed.

CHAPTER 14

In his lair, the Toymaker watched Juni through a hologram. His three trusted advisors surrounded him.

"He's good. The boy warrior is very good," the advisor who was dressed like a cruel dictator observed.

"But he has to keep going—this game is not easy," the clever one said. "The game is a challenge, yes. The Toymaker made it so . . . but the boy must get to the end."

Now the good and sensitive advisor spoke. "He must not give up. Not slow down." The advisor looked at the Toymaker. "He must get to the end, and you will be free, Toymaker."

The Clever Advisor looked concerned. "How can we help him?"

The Dictator Advisor gave the Good Advisor

a stern look. "We can't help—it's not part of the game!"

All three advisors swayed and took in the words that were just spoken. The rules of the game were set and final.

The Toymaker paced and tried to remain calm. He hated being left out of the conversation! He began to mutter to himself. "I don't mind talking to myself. But when you guys start cutting me out of the conversation, that's when it's a little strange."

The advisors looked at one another and did not say another word.

"That's it!" The Toymaker suddenly proclaimed. "More life is what we need. Grant the boy a gift . . . the gift of life!"

The advisors all smiled and nodded in agreement. The Toymaker was helping the boy. The three advisors raised their hands and high-fived one another.

◎ ◎ ◎

Juni received his gift almost immediately. He was walking along with the others when a bonus Life Pack suddenly appeared in front of him. *BANG!* He hit his head against it and fell to the ground.

The other kids helped him up. "You all right,

Guy?" Francis asked. Then he noticed what Juni had walked into. "You found a Life Pack!" he cheered.

"A what?" said Juni, still a little woozy from the head-bonking he had just received.

"Bonus Life Pack," Rez put in. "That's rare. Never seen one up close before." The kids handed it over to Juni.

"All yours, Guy," Francis said. "Congratulations."

"What do I do?" Juni wanted to know.

"Crush it in your hands," Arnold explained. "You'll gain life."

"How much?" Juni asked.

"All depends," said Francis.

Juni thought for a minute, then walked over to Demetra.

The group didn't notice but the Toymaker lurked behind them, watching. He shook his head. "Oh boy, just throw my gift away, kid," he said.

"I've got extra life, Demetra," Juni announced.

"Congratulations," said Demetra. "You'll need it most."

"I want *you* to take it," Juni said, trying to put it in her hand

Demetra pulled away. "Juni, I can't," she protested.

Juni was a little hurt, but he shook it off. "Suit

yourself," he said with a shrug. Then he crushed the Life Pack in his hand and tossed it at her feet. It exploded, sending a warm electrical glow over her. Her life counter clicked up fifteen points. Everyone gasped.

Francis shook his head in disbelief. "You just gave her *fifteen* life points," he said. "You know what that's worth?"

Rez leaned over. "Of course he does," he said to Francis.

"I owed you from the Arena of Misfortune," Juni told Demetra. "Also," he said, blushing, "I don't want anything to happen to you."

Demetra smiled. "Well, if it does, I'll be ready now, won't I?" Then she added softly, "Thank you."

Juni gave Demetra a big goofy grin in return.

◎ ◎ ◎

"*YOU HAVE NOW ENTERED LEVEL THREE,*" the computer said. There was a lot of hand slapping and congratulations all around. Back at OSS Headquarters, everyone was cheering.

"We're only on Level Three," Cesca said, the voice of reason. "It's only Level Three."

"What are you talking about?" Donnagon demanded. "They've practically got this game won!" He laughed with glee, crumpling up the printout he was reading and tossing it up over his head in victory. It knocked into the face of an agent in one of the upper cubicles, who fell to the ground, smashing up the place. *CRASH!*

Donnagon made a face. Nothing was going to mess with his good mood.

CHAPTER 15

Level Three was a beautiful sight to see.

Arnold looked around in awe. "I wish my family could see this amazing place," he said.

Juni realized he hardly knew anything about the people he was entrusting with his very lives. "What are you doing in here?" he asked Arthur. "Why are you in the game?"

It was a sad story. "My parents' couldn't afford to buy me this game," Arnold said. "I got it on a beta tester's Visa."

Juni leaned forward, listening.

"An opportunity to offer diversity amongst players," Francis explained.

"I'm here for the great prize behind Level Five," Arnold said shyly. "It will save my family from poverty." He looked up. "What waits for us in Level

Five? Is it all true? Untold riches? Toys and games beyond our wildest dreams?"

Juni felt sick to his stomach. "Untold riches," he said softly. "Yeah."

"I know," said Arnold understandingly. "You can't really say. But I can tell you know what's really there. I can't wait to see for myself."

Juni was silent. Then he finally spoke. "Arnold, you should know that when we reach the end of the game . . ."

"Don't tell me," Arnold interrupted. "I want it to be a surprise."

Juni took a deep breath. "I'm sure it will be," was all he said.

"*Attention, Gamers!*" the Toymaker's voice boomed. "Stand on the red line."

Everyone obeyed the command.

"We can take it," added Francis.

"*Choose your best player,*" the Toymaker said.

No question. The group chose Juni. He stepped forward.

"*Choose your strongest player,*" the Toymaker continued.

No question there either. "That'd be Arnold," said Rez.

Arnold smiled proudly and flexed his muscles.

Two glowing staffs were tossed to Juni and Arnold. They hoisted them above their shoulders, assuming their fighting stance against the computer.

"Let's take 'em, Guy," said Arnold confidently.

Juni nodded.

"Battle round! Face your opponent now!" the Toymaker's voice said.

Huh? Juni looked around. Nothing there.

"FACE YOUR OPPONENT!" the voice insisted.

What was going on? "Where *is* the opponent?" said Juni.

Suddenly, with a sinking feeling in his stomach, it all made sense to Juni. The ground that he and Arnold were standing on began to shift, and soon, the two were facing off against—each other!

"Wait a minute," protested Juni. "I'm not fighting Arnold."

Arnold made a face. "I don't want to crush Juni!" he cried.

"The battle is irreversible," said the Toymaker. *"The winner shall proceed with the others to Level Four. The loser shall be given an immediate 'Game Over' and will be evacuated permanently from the game."*

Juni looked at Arnold pleadingly. "Arnold, please," he begged. "I have to save my sister."

The look on Arnold's face almost broke Juni's heart. He was visibly torn—between loyalty to The Guy, and his own family. But winning the game, and its untold riches, was a necessity for him. "I'm sorry, Juni," he finally said. "But I have my own family to think about, you know."

The ground broke away, and Juni and Arnold were led out to fight their battle—alone. Juni turned back to face the others. They all looked back mutely. Nobody knew what to say.

Francis finally broke the silence. "Tough game," he said simply.

Visibly shaken, Arnold managed to steel himself and assume the fighting stance. Juni reluctantly did the same. He looked Arnold square in the eye. "I can't beat you," he said.

"I know," Arnold replied. He threw the first strike, connected, and sent Juni hurtling into a sphere. It spun and rotated, throwing him off balance. Juni regained his footing and struck back. He looked down. There was no floor beneath them, just shifting shapes. As they battled they constantly went flying from shape to shape, which turned and flipped. It was almost impossible to keep their balance.

The fight got more and more intense. I can't win, Juni kept thinking. I just can't win. It looked like it was 'Game Over' for him when he got struck by Arnold's staff and lost a life. Arnold kicked him.

Juni lost a life. Arnold swung at him and connected. Juni lost another life.

Three . . . two . . . one . . . every time Juni checked his life meter it was dwindling down lower and lower. This can't be happening, he thought. But it was. The next time Arnold landed a blow, Juni's life meter clicked down to .5!

"It was nice knowing you," said Arnold, ready to aim the final blow.

"*Adiós, amigo.*"

And suddenly, unexpectedly, the game halted. Arnold's staff shut off.

The ground split apart, and Juni was led back to the others.

"What's going on?" Juni wondered.

"*You've been tagged,*" said the Toymaker.

Juni was confused. "What do you mean, 'I've been tagged?'"

"*Someone has switched places with you,*" the Toymaker told him.

Juni stepped off the platform and looked at Rez quizzically.

"Not me, Guy," said Rez.

But who could it be? Who was brave enough to face off against Arnold? Juni turned around to see Demetra on the platform being led over to fight.

What was going on? "Demetra, what are you doing?" he called.

"You have to find your sister, Juni," she answered back.

This was wrong—all wrong! "Don't do it!"

Demetra ignored him and caught a glowing staff. Arnold's came back to life. He resumed the fighting stance, but it was clear his heart wasn't in it.

"Demetra, no!" Juni shouted.

"Maybe we'll meet again," Demetra said bravely. "In some other game."

"*Fight*," the Toymaker commanded.

"Noooooo!" Juni cried.

Demetra struck at Arnold, who parried. His staff blasted open the platform. And Demetra began to fall.

"Save your sister, Juni!" she cried.

In midair, her image suddenly zapped out completely. Demetra was gone. Her game was most definitely over.

Overcome, Juni fell to his knees in grief. Rez reached over and patted his back. Arnold rejoined the group. He could barely meet Juni's gaze. "I'm sorry, Juni," he said softly. "My family . . ."

Juni sighed deeply. "I never even got . . . her e-mail address," he finished.

A giant metal hand gripped his shoulder. "Don't fall in love with the game, Juni," said Valentin.

Juni stood and wiped his eyes. Looking up at

the scoreboard he saw that Demetra's name had been erased completely.

"Let's get out of here," Juni said. Without a moment of hesitation he charged toward the Level Four door up ahead. Valentin fell into step beside his grandson.

"As I was trying to tell you, Juni," he said, "the only way to really stop this game is to stop the Toymaker."

Valentin stared at the butterfly in his hands and whispered quietly. "You are causing so much pain. Only I can stop you. For I know why you do these things, Toymaker."

◎ ◎ ◎

The Toymaker watched the tender family scene through his hologram. He nodded his head in agreement.

"Bring it on. Find me and the world will truly pay the price," he said. "Here in my cyber prison . . . I've been forced to create. Now I will destroy."

The Toymaker stood and addressed his advisors. "Release her. Put her back in the game."

"But, sir," the Good Advisor argued.

"You have a better solution?" asked the Toymaker. Then he laughed. "Of course, you all do. Tell me. What is the real answer?"

Three holographic advisors stepped forward.

"Revenge," said one.

"Healing," said another.

"Destruction," a third said, quite cheerfully.

The Toymaker surveyed his creations. "Once again, you're all correct. And once again, you're all incorrect." He reached over and shut them all off. Next, he released Carmen. She woke up, looked around wildly for a moment, realized where she was, and then disappeared from the sphere.

"On with the game, my dear," the Toymaker said with a small smile.

CHAPTER 16

"*You are now entering Level Four,*" a computerized voice said as the huge doors swung open.

"Level Four?" said Juni excitedly. "Wait a minute. Carmen is on this level!"

Everyone looked out in dismay at the expansive, impossible landscape.

"I'll use telepathy," Juni said decisively. "We might be close enough. That'll work."

Juni walked out onto a ledge. A vast chasm yawned underneath it, but he barely noticed. He closed his eyes and squeezed his temples. *Carmen, Carmen, can you . . .*

WHAT? Carmen replied so loudly it made Juni jump. His ears ringing, he nodded to Valentin.

"It . . . uh . . . works," he said. He pressed his temples again. He wanted to be sure this was really and truly his sister.

This game plays tricks, he thought. *Say something only Carmen would say.*

Carmen didn't even need to think. She answered immediately. *MY FEET STINK!*

Juni lowered his hands. It *was* Carmen! *You sound close*, he thought.

"I am," Carmen replied out loud. Juni spun around.

And there she was—right behind him, looking battle scarred but super cool with the light shining behind her.

Juni smiled.

◎ ◎ ◎

On the way to Lava Mountain, Carmen pulled Juni aside. "You brought Grandpa into the game?" she asked.

Juni shrugged. "I thought it was a good idea at the time," he explained.

"We can't let him know the Toymaker is behind this . . ." Carmen began.

"He already knows," Juni replied.

Carmen's jaw dropped. "Juni, the Toymaker is the man who put Grandpa in a wheelchair thirty years ago!"

This piece of information stopped Juni dead in his tracks.

"If Grandpa tries to take revenge," Carmen

explained, "the Toymaker will break free. He's *that* powerful."

"We have to tell Grandpa that revenge is not the way to solve this," said Juni.

"Good idea," Carmen said. Then, "You tell him."

Before Juni could reply, Rez, Francis, and Arnold approached them.

"Okay, Guy," Rez said to Juni. "You found your pal. Now where are we going exactly? Where's Level Five?"

Juni opened his mouth to speak but Carmen jumped right in. She had no time for these guys and she wasn't afraid to let them know it.

"First of all," she began, "you don't ask the questions around here, I do. Second of all . . ."

"We're going to Lava Mountain," finished Juni.

Carmen looked at her brother challengingly. "We are?"

Juni pulled out Demetra's map and tried to show it to Carmen. "Beyond that is the passage to Level Five," he said, pointing. But she wasn't paying attention.

"I don't think so," retorted Carmen.

Rez and Francis were indignant.

"So suddenly *you're* The Guy expert?" said Rez.

"We're following The Guy!" protested Francis, pointing at Juni.

But it only took one look to put them in their place. Carmen grabbed Juni and pulled him aside again. "You know, Juni," she said in a low voice. "We don't need these guys following us. Not where we're going."

"I promised they could tag along," Juni argued. He pulled out the map again. "This is how I know where to go. Trust me."

Juni leaned in closer to Carmen. "A friend of mine lost her life—her game life—getting this. I have to follow it."

"Do they even know what we're up to?" Carmen asked. "That we're going to destroy the game after Level Five?"

"Of course," Juni fibbed. "Come on, let's just get there, okay?"

Carmen looked over at the kids. They were watching her and Juni's every move.

"If you want me to take care of them," Carmen said. "I can take care of them. No problem."

"Let's go, Carmen," said Juni. "Let's go, guys."

Rez, Francis, and Arnold followed along, giving them suspicious glances. The dynamic had definitely changed. The trust was gone. Everyone eyed each other with suspicion.

"This game isn't fun anymore," Juni muttered to himself.

CHAPTER 17

After walking for a while, they approached an incredible mountain of lava. Waves of red hot molten stuff crashed around them. The surf was up, but *nobody* wanted to get in!

"Lava Mountain," said Carmen.

Juni groaned. "Why is it that every video game has lava in it?" he wanted to know.

"Well, technically that's not true," explained Carmen, surveying the stuff. "There's no lava in HALO. And in METROID, it's molten magma."

"What?" said Rez.

"I've got six lives left!" argued Arnold.

"Doesn't matter," Carmen said firmly. "If you fall in, 'Game Over.'"

Juni couldn't believe his ears. "That's insane," he said.

"Not even one drop?" asked Francis hopefully.

"Not even one drop," confirmed Carmen. "The game's getting tougher, guys."

Juni felt defeated. "Carmen, this is impossible," he said, his shoulders sagging.

Carmen looked at her little brother. "This was your call, sport." She stared at the lava, deep in thought.

"What do you think?" she asked, turning to Grandpa.

"Difficult," Valentin said simply.

That was all Carmen needed to hear. "You're right. Let's go another way," she decided.

Whew! Rez, Francis, and Arnold breathed a sigh of relief. But Juni took out the map again. "Doesn't make sense," he said.

◎ ◎ ◎

The Toymaker was furious. "I give them a map!" he fumed. "I give them a path—what more do they want! Can't just lead them to the door!"

"Impossible!" stated his Clever Advisor. "When Carmen the Agent released the virus into the system, an AI was implanted so you couldn't escape."

"I know, I KNOW!" The Toymaker groaned. "Let me talk to myself at least!"

"You *are* talking to yourself," said the Good Advisor. "I *am* you."

The Toymaker had had enough. He looked

sternly at the advisors. "Well, then—you, me—SHUT UP!"

"Yes, sir," responded the Good Advisor politely.

The Toymaker looked up. The whole absurdity of the situation was getting to him.

"*Am* I insane?" he wondered out loud.

"Completely," replied the Dictator Advisor.

The Toymaker quickly pushed a button, causing the dictator to disappear.

"Oh, shut up," the Toymaker said. He wound up his toy bird and set it down. Its wings flapped up and down.

He retuned his gaze to the hologram. "They're going the wrong way!" he complained. "I have to drive them to Level Five." He opened a panel revealing a whole new set of buttons. He pushed one. "Send in the Tinkertoys!" he cried.

◎ ◎ ◎

As the group walked away from the lava, Rez said to Juni, "This is good thinking. She's good, Guy. We should listen to her more often."

"Stay off my side," Carmen snapped.

"Okay," Rez said meekly.

Suddenly the ground in front of them started to lift.

"What is this?" cried Carmen.

Everyone watched in disbelief as a bunch of

freaky-looking metallic heads began poking up through the ground. One came up directly under Arnold and lifted him into the air. Francis quickly thumbed through his rule book, trying to identify the strange creatures. "Tinkertoys!" he cried.

Tinkertoys! Everyone bolted back the way they had come.

"Wait!" shouted Juni. "What's worse? Lava or Tinkertoys?"

Francis didn't have to think twice. *"Definitely* Tinkertoys!" he shouted.

Everyone began to sprint, the Tinkertoys hot on their heels.

"Carmen, what do we do?" Juni said, panting.

Carmen did an instantaneous survey and made a split-second decision. "Use the flat rocks as surfboards!" she shouted. "It's our only chance!"

Everyone leaped up onto the nearby flat rocks. The force of their weight broke them off, and they landed in the terribly dangerous lava. The surf was up and the waves were certainly not tasty. They were red hot!

"Stick together!" Carmen shouted as they headed for the first lava cliff. Immediately a drop of lava splashed onto Juni's suit and began eating through the material.

"Arggh!" Juni groaned. He started spitting on himself to put out the fire.

The Tinkertoys stood at the edge of the lava, unsure of what to do. Then one by one they began to leap right into the lava. Immediately they popped back out, transformed into Lava Choads. They gave chase on fiery surfboards.

Juni shook his head. He couldn't believe this was actually happening!

◎ ◎ ◎

Back at OSS headquarters, Cesca was flabbergasted. "What are they doing?" she said.

"They're straying from the path," said Donnagon. "Carmen led them away but they got chased back to Lava Mountain. I think the Toymaker figured out a way to escape. He must be pushing them toward his lair."

Cesca stared at her husband. "But why?" she mused. "What could he possibly gain from . . ." Just then she saw Valentin, surfing away. "What's the connection between Juni's grandfather and the Toymaker, if any?" she asked the agents.

The staff began to pound the keyboards looking for the answer.

"Hurry, people," Cesca said in a warning tone.

"Coming onscreen," someone said.

Valentin and the Toymaker popped up on the screen. Comrades turned enemies. *Bitter* enemies.

"Toymaker's counting on Valentin to break him out of the game," said Donnagon. "And he may just succeed."

"Stop them," said Cesca. "Throw in a lava monster. Stop the lava. Bigger waves—anything. We have to create obstacles for them."

"We have to drown them," stated Donnagon flatly.

Cesca glared at her husband.

"They'll get an immediate 'Game Over' and be evacuated from the game," he explained.

Cesca was thinking. Donnagon's hand hovered near the button.

"We can't risk letting the Toymaker out," he reminded her.

Cesca grimaced, but made the call. "Do it," she said.

Donnagon did.

Juni's spit technique had put out his flaming suit but he soon had bigger problems to contend with. The lava waves were getting bigger and stronger, and the Choads began lobbing fireballs at them.

"Encircle The Guy!" Rez shouted. "We have to protect him!"

"Why do they keep calling you that?" Carmen wanted to know.

"Long story!" Juni yelled back over his shoulder.

Valentin turned to face the Choads. "I'll hold them off," he said. "Continue to the other side."

Juni hated it when the group split up. It never worked! Never ever! "Grandpa, no, stay with the group!" he shouted.

But Valentin would not listen. He sailed to the top of a lava rock. The Choads attacked Valentin, pouring over him in a river of molten lava.

"Grandpa!" Juni screamed.

He turned to Carmen, but she was busy looking up ahead. From her expression he could tell that she saw something. Something bad.

"What is . . ." he began.

"Don't ask," Carmen replied. For ahead of them was a monstrous fifty-story lava creature. It reached down and threw a giant flaming lava rock at them. Arnold was the first to be hit.

"Arnold!" Juni cried as Arnold slipped under the lava.

"What's going on?" Rez asked, confused.

"I don't know," Juni told him.

BAM! Rez was hit next. Down he went.

"You really did it this time, Guy!" said Francis.
Juni protested. "But I didn't . . ."

WHACK! Francis was next.

Juni was panicking. "Carmen!" he called.

She swooped her rockboard over next to Juni. "What do we do?" he asked.

"We have to defeat the Boss! The Lava Choad in charge!" she explained.

If only it were that easy! "How?" Juni said.

WHACK! Carmen was hit . . . hard. She flew high above her board. Thinking quickly, Juni surfed up a wall, broke off another rock, and flung it into the lava—right under his sister. *WHEW!*

"Thanks, Juni!" Carmen called. But her new board began to crack. Then the Lava Boss tossed one last chunk at her. *SMACK!* Score—direct hit. Carmen went under.

"I'm coming!" shouted Juni, surfing to her side as quickly as he could. As Carmen was pulled under she reached up her hand for help. He got to her just in time to see her hand disappear.

Juni was furious. Searching so long for his sister only to have her taken away so suddenly! Now he was all alone again. No Valentin. No Carmen. No one at all.

The Lava Boss continued to hurl flaming chunks at him, causing giant spurts of lava to shoot up around him. Juni surfed over a lava spurt and was lifted high into the air. "I hate this game. I hate this game!" he shouted.

In a fit of anger, he turned his board so it was aimed directly at the Boss, hitting him and bursting right though his chest. The creature bent over, reached down, and picked up a fireball. Juni knew this one had his name on it.

BOOM! Direct hit! Juni flew right over a cliff. A huge lava pool spread out beneath him.

"I hate this game . . ." Juni said one last time, right before he was swallowed up by the lava.

CHAPTER 18

"Where are they?" Cesca asked worriedly.

"They went in," confirmed Donnagon.

"I know, but they should have gotten a 'Game Over.' They should be back here, actually," she said.

Donnagon looked around. His wife was right. . . .

◎ ◎ ◎

Juni floated through the thick red lava, knocked out cold. Suddenly a garbled voice snapped him into consciousness.

"This way! Juni! This way!" a voice was saying. It sounded like Carmen!

Juni looked around. He wasn't on fire, he was underwater. Under thick red water to be exact. And it was actually a little cold!

He looked down. Carmen was below, waving for him to follow. She was near an open door. Juni watched as the others swam through it. Juni kicked, and swam through too.

◎ ◎ ◎

Juni looked around. They were in the Toymaker's underground lair!

"I thought I was a goner," said Rez, spitting lava.

"I saw all my points flashing away before my eyes," confessed Arnold. "And all I could hear was my father saying, 'You blew it, Arnold. *No untold riches for you!*'"

Lava shot out of Francis's ears. He was reading his tech manual and eyeing Juni.

Juni had his eyes on Carmen. She was holding a piece of Grandpa's suit.

"Where's Grandpa?" Juni asked, walking over to Carmen.

"I don't know," Carmen said. "But he isn't here." She examined the piece of the suit in her hand. "Isn't this a piece of his armor?"

Juni wasn't listening anymore. He was focused on what he saw ahead of them. It was a large strange stone slab. "Carmen!" he said. "It's a door. Help me open it."

Carmen followed Juni to the stone slab. Then

using her enhanced arm, she tried to unlock the secret entrance.

Meanwhile, Francis was busy reading the tech manual and getting more information about the game. He walked over to Rez. "Red flag, Rez," he said. "We have to talk about The Guy. Highly sensitive," he added, making sure that no one else was listening.

"What about him?" asked Rez.

"I've been rereading the tech manual. It speaks of an infidel within the game. Designed to mislead you down a path where no one will survive. I think . . ." He looked around. "I think Juni's a Deceiver."

Rez was starting to get nervous. "What do you suggest?"

"If he's a Deceiver, we'll have to get rid of him. Or risk losing the game," answered Francis.

"What about his sister?" asked Rez. He kind of liked Carmen. She was smart, feisty, and cute.

"Her too," said Francis solemnly.

Juni watched as Carmen worked the door with her electric arm. A loose rock was the key and the rocks disappeared.

"It's the door to Level Five!" Juni exclaimed. "If only we could figure out how to open it."

"How much time do we have left?" Carmen asked.

Juni looked at his watch. "Five minutes," he answered.

The three beta testers walked over to join the Spy Kids.

"What happens in five minutes?" Rez asked.

"This place gets flooded with players from around the world," said Carmen.

"Oh, great," said Francis. "Competition."

"They won't know it's a game, and the Toymaker will take over their minds," said Carmen. "That's what the mind-control feature of the game is. You lose all perspective. That's why we have to shut down the game."

Oh no! Carmen had just let the cat out of the bag! "Shhh . . . Carmen," Juni said warningly.

"What do you mean, *shut it down*?" Rez said, his voice rising. "What's she talking about?"

Carmen turned to Juni. "You didn't tell them? Did you?"

"Deceivers," Francis hissed.

Arnold looked devastated. "What about the other side of Level Five?" he asked. "Riches beyond imagining, right, Juni?"

"There *is* no other side," said Carmen. "All that happens when you get there is 'Game Over.' There's nothing afterward. You will be imprisoned in the game, and the Toymaker will rule what's left of your life. The End."

Arnold looked at Juni, his eyes wide with disbelief. "You lied to us to get your way, Juni? You lied?"

Rez, Francis, and Arnold began to approach Juni menacingly. "We're not letting you shut this game down, Juni. And now you're gonna see just how fast that counter of yours can count backward," Rez said threateningly.

"You've gotta get through me first, Game Boy," said Carmen.

"Now listen to me." Juni tried to calm Arnold down. "I'm The Guy."

"Stop saying you are The Guy," Rez said. "We know you're not The Guy."

Everyone raised their fists. Carmen swung her arm back, ready to defend her brother. Then suddenly . . .

"HE'S NOT THE GUY!" a voice shouted.

They all turned around, openmouthed.

"I AM," the voice said.

CHAPTER 19

Everyone whipped around. And out of the blinding light came a shape, which soon formed into, well, a guy.

"And you are?" said Rex.

"I'm The Guy," said The Guy. He was dressed in a sharp suit made of polished chrome.

"The *real* Guy," he continued. "And I say we go in, we beat this unwinnable game, and we get to the other side. Where untold riches and a bounty fit for *ten* kings awaits us!"

"I knew it!" said Arnold happily.

Francis nodded "Now, *he's* definitely The Guy," he said.

"But it's unwinnable," Carmen argued.

The Guy gave her a look that was amazingly piercing, yet filled with complete understanding and compassion. Then he crouched on the ground. Everyone crouched down, too.

The Guy spoke softly. "Nothing is unwinnable—if we all join forces and battle as one. We play on one another's strengths and help cover one another's weaknesses."

They all looked at each other. This Guy was cool.

"We can accomplish anything. And we *will* accomplish everything. But first . . ." He stood up. ". . . Let's go whip this unwinnable level and show it who's boss!"

The others just stared, speechless.

"Are you with me?" he asked.

"Yeah!" everyone cheered, standing up, ready to follow The Guy into the unwinnable level and kick it to kingdom come.

The Guy spun around and aimed his hand at the door to Level Five. It flew open as if it were built out of matchsticks.

"Ooohhh," everyone said in unison.

The Guy strode forward into the unwinnable level confidently. Rez, Francis, Arnold, Valentin, Carmen, and Juni followed.

BOOM! A giant lightning bolt shot out of the grid and struck The Guy full in the chest. It sent him flying back, and he fell to the floor, skidding into a wall.

"Oh, my," said Rez. They huddled around him and watched in disbelief as his lives counted down. 99, 98, 97, 96 . . . all the way down to .5.

"Oops," said The Guy. "Game Over." *POOF!* He disappeared in a cloud of smoke.

"Guy!" said Francis sorrowfully.

Everyone stared at Juni. "Okay, you're The Guy again," said Rez resignedly. "Get us through this, Juni."

"But I . . ." Juni started to say. Then he looked up and saw—could it be—

"Demetra!" he shouted.

"Juni, quickly!" she cried. "I found the switch to shut the game down. I also found the exit portal. We can all get out of here right now!"

"How did you find us? How did you survive?" Juni wanted to know.

She brushed his question off. "There was a glitch in the game—I don't know. Maybe it was that extra Life Pack you gave me. But I'm here now, and I know the way out."

Carmen stepped up, her eyes narrowed and her arms crossed. "Juni, who is this?" she asked.

"Follow me, Juni. Quickly!" Demetra insisted.

"This is Demetra," explained Juni. "My girl . . . my friend . . . she's my . . ."

"I'm his girlfriend," said Demetra. "Who are you?"

"I'm his sister," said Carmen. She took a closer look at Demetra and frowned. "Juni, she's not real."

"What are you talking about?" Demetra cried. "I've been helping Juni win the game. What have *you* been doing? Playing prisoner, that's what. And doing a good job of it!"

"She gave me the map," said Juni. "The map that got us . . . here . . ." He broke off and looked at Demetra.

Carmen gave him a tight smile. "She set you up, Juni. Set us all up."

Demetra turned to Juni. "Please, Juni! She's lying!" she insisted. "She's been the Toymaker's prisoner. She could be brainwashed for all we know. Do you want to win this game or not?"

Carmen swung her arm at Demetra. And it passed right through her!

Juni couldn't believe it. Demetra wasn't real! He slowly reached for her.

"Don't," Demetra said, turning away. Juni's hand went right through her holographic face.

"Don't touch me," she said softly.

"She's the reason this level is unwinnable, Juni. She's the Deceiver. Everything she told you is a lie," said Carmen.

Demetra looked crestfallen. "I'm sorry, Juni,

but . . . it's in my programming," she explained with a sigh.

The ominous sound of many doors slamming shut at once echoed through the chamber. They were locked in.

"Why?" Juni asked sadly.

"Only the Toymaker knows," said Demetra. "He led you here."

"We're trapped," said Rez.

Giant robots began to rise from the floor around them.

"*Congratulations*," the Toymaker's voice boomed.

Everyone turned around and watched the Toymaker looking down on them on the hologram table. He was larger than large!

"You've made it to the end of the game. You've won!" The Toymaker raved. "Untold riches for all of you! And the prize is . . . you get to stay here . . . forever, and ever, and ever!"

"Juni! This way!" Valentin shouted.

Juni turned to see Valentin holding open a portal.

"This is the way out! All of you, quickly!" Valentin yelled.

Everyone ran to the portal and began climbing out. But Juni stopped.

"Wait, we have to shut down the game," he said.

"I already did!" Valentin said. "The switch is right there."

Juni looked over and saw two switches. One was flipped down.

"Are you sure?" Juni asked warily.

"Yes!" Valentin replied impatiently. "Go inside, *quickly!*"

Juni turned to see the monstrous robots crawling out of the grid, like zombies from the grave. Juni rushed to the portal.

"Run, Grandpa!" Juni shouted.

Demetra grabbed the portal.

"Go," she said to Valentin. "I'll hold it open."

Valentin let go. Demetra turned to Juni.

"Go now," she said.

"Demetra . . ." Juni began.

"I can't hold it open forever," responded Demetra, looking away.

The robots began reaching over Demetra toward him. Juni leaped inside the portal. The door shut, trapping one of the robot's monstrous hands inside, still grabbing for Juni.

Juni and Valentin ran down the portal. There was an exit door at the end. The kids stood in front of it exchanging e-mail addresses.

"Thanks for everything, Guy," said Francis.

"It was real," said Rez, then caught himself. "Sort of. I guess."

Arnold gave Juni a crushing handshake. "Thank you," he said softly.

Arnold, Rez, and Francis all leaped through the exit, followed by Carmen. Juni was poised to go next when Valentin spoke.

"I'll catch up to you, Juni," he said. "There is unfinished business I have to attend to."

"The Toymaker is defeated," Juni protested. "We don't have to do anything else."

Valentin looked away.

A sudden realization dawned on Juni. "You don't *want* to leave, do you?" he asked.

Valentin turned back to face Juni. He stood tall—strong and proud.

"How can I go back, Juni?" he asked sadly.

Juni felt panicked. They were running out of time. They had to get out of there—right away! And he couldn't leave his grandfather behind.

"In here I can walk, I can run," explained Valentin. "You look at me like I'm some sort of . . . superhero."

"You are!" Juni said. "Out there in the *real* world . . . to me . . . you are."

"Am I?" Valentin asked. "Am I really?"

"In here," Juni said, "it's not real."

Juni took his grandfather's big strong hand, and Valentin let go of the butterfly he was holding. Juni and Valentin both watched it flutter away.

"Don't fall in love with the game," Juni reminded him.

"Okay, Juni, I will return," Valentin said slowly. "If you promise me that even through I'll be in a wheelchair, that you look at me no differently than you are now. Because on the *inside*, Juni . . . on the *inside* . . ."

A smile broke out on Valentin's face. ". . . I feel . . . like this."

Valentin began to dance. He flipped in the air. He even did some splits. Juni watched him, feeling a bit sad.

"I promise, Grandpa," said Juni.

Valentin nodded. "Time to go."

Lifting Juni in his strong arms, Valentin carried him through the exit door at the end of the portal.

CHAPTER 20

Back in OSS Headquarters, Juni removed his glasses and rubbed his eyes.

"Those video games are killer on the eyes, huh, kid?" said Donnagon.

Juni looked over and saw his grandfather back in his wheelchair. He grabbed the handles and pushed him forward. Agents gathered around, applauding them.

"Coming through, coming through, please," said Valentin.

Donnagon reached over to take the wheelchair from Juni. "We'll take it from here, Juni," he said.

"My grandson can handle it," Valentin said. "Don't touch. This is Corinthian leather."

Donnagon and Cesca began debriefing the group.

"Tell me again how you shut off the game," Donnagon asked.

Juni looked at Carmen.

"I don't know if we shut it down exactly," Carmen admitted. "We hit a switch, and it seemed to work."

"Oh, it worked," said Cesca. "The game is down. We just need to make sure we did this correctly."

Juni thought for a moment. "I don't know," he said. "I think Grandpa hit the switch actually."

Donnagon turned to Valentin. "Let's have it, Valentin. What switch did you hit, exactly? There were two switches side by side. One shuts down the game, one reverses the virus, releasing the Toymaker. Did you shut down the game? Or did you free the Toymaker by accident?"

Valentin sat up straighter in his wheelchair. "I *did* free the Toymaker," he said coolly. "But it was no accident."

Juni and Carmen stood in stunned silence.

"If you want to end the game," Valentin explained, "you have to defeat the Toymaker. It's the only way."

Donnagon stared in shock. "You crazy old man!" he exploded.

"Do you know what you've done?" Cesca moaned.

Juni turned to his grandfather. "Grandpa, revenge doesn't solve anything."

Valentin looked deep into Juni's eyes. "Will you trust me?" he asked. "You of all people?"

Juni gulped.

Just then the presidential seal appeared on the monitors.

"Message from the president?" Donnagon wondered out loud. "What does he want?"

"I'm coming back," a voice said. "To settle the score. For imprisoning me. For using me."

"Devlin?" Carmen said incredulously. "*Devlin* set us up?"

"It's not Devlin," Juni said, his heart sinking.

The monitor crackled with static, and the true speaker appeared. The Toymaker.

"I wanted to right the wrongs," he said. "Start again. A new world. A new chance. *Everyone* would get a second chance. So now . . . I'm taking this to the next level."

Alarms began to wail and long sheets of paper began to shoot out of the OSS printers.

"Why did you let him out?" Donnagon cried.

"Because only *I* can stop him!" Valentin shouted.

"Seismic activity is off the map!" an agent reported. "Earthquakes. Tornadoes. Hurricanes."

"Can you stop *that*?" Donnagon cried.

◎ ◎ ◎

Juni ran outside the office. The buildings were swaying and the ground was shaking. This was bad. Very bad. His 3-D glasses still in his hand, he raised them to his face. And suddenly he could see what was going on. This was no earthquake— there were giant robots roaming through the streets!

"Quick, Carmen, put these on!" he shouted. "It's the only way to see what's really happening!" he explained.

She put them on.

One . . . two . . . three . . . make that *ten* robots were roaming the city, destroying things in their path, and jumping up and down on the ground like giant metal toddlers having a tantrum. The cars bounced up and down like tiny Matchbox cars. The robots were bent on destruction of everything and anything OSS.

"We're doomed," said Juni.

Carmen remained calm. "Only one thing to do in a situation like this," she said. "Call in the family."

Call in the family! *Right!* "Of course," said Juni. "Why didn't I think of that?"

Carmen lifted her wristwatch to her mouth and hit a button. "Calling all Cortezes," she said.

◎ ◎ ◎

Gregorio Cortez was in a hidden OSS laboratory, working on an elaborate brain project that was top secret.

"This is it . . . this is it . . . this is it!" he crowed as he probed the brain with instruments. "The moment we've all been waiting for. Nobody move, nobody move. Nobody touch the brain. The fifth brain. This is probably . . . no . . . this IS the most important moment of my entire life. I must activate it *right now*."

An assistant nervously approached him. "Sir?"

"Eh?" Gregorio said, not looking up.

"Your children called," the assistant continued. "They said it's an emergency."

Before the assistant even finished the sentence, Dad leaped out of his seat, knocking over the fifth brain in the process. It smashed to the ground, breaking into a thousand pieces. Then Dad leaped off the table, activating his rocket boots. He soared up and out of the skylight like Superman.

Felix walked in, saw the destroyed fifth brain on the floor, and dropped his notebook. "Well, I'm their uncle!" he said. He clicked his heels and blasted off, leaving the assistants behind in a cloud of Jet Shoe Smoke.

Dad landed on the ground in front of Juni and Carmen, his coat billowing in the wind. Very action-hero.

"Where are they?" he asked.

Juni pulled out an extra pair of glasses. "You'll need these to see them!" he explained.

"LOOK OUT!" Carmen shouted. For behind Gregorio was a giant robot, about to crush him like a bug! Quickly, Gregorio pulled a light pen out of his pocket. The giant foot then stomped down on him!

"DAAAAAD!" yelled Juni.

The robot had a grimace on its face, which then turned into a look of surprise. A circle was being cut out of its foot. The top popped off like a manhole cover, and there stood Gregorio, brandishing his laser pen. The confused robot lifted his foot up to take a look at the giant hole.

"Glasses, quick!" Gregorio shouted.

Carmen tossed him a pair of glasses with the smooth moves of a ninja. They landed perfectly on his face.

Gregorio leaped up and grabbed onto the robot's foot. He climbed on and ran up its leg. He began to fight, as best he could with a metal creature a dozen times his own height. He flew up and around the creature, conking it in the face.

Just then Ingrid, Helga, and Machete landed. Felix plopped down in Machete's arms. Machete tossed him to his feet.

"Mom! Uncle Machete!" Carmen cried.

"Grandma! Uncle Felix!" shouted Juni.

"So what are we looking at here?" Machete said.

Carmen tossed three pairs of glasses at them with the same fluid motion as before. *WHOOSH. WHOOSH. WHOOSH.*

"Oh!" said Machete, seeing the robots. "Oh," he said, more softly.

"This . . . won't be easy," said Helga.

"Where's your father?" Ingrid asked.

"Up there," said Juni, pointing. Dad was struggling, stuck in the robot's vise like grip.

"Machete! Felix! Mom! Let's kick some metal," said Ingrid.

"How?" asked Felix.

Ingrid thought for a moment. "I have an idea. Climb!"

She began to shimmy up the robot's leg.

Down on the ground, the situation looked grim.

"What about all those other ones?" asked Carmen.

"We need more help!" said Juni, looking around wildly. "Our family's not big enough."

Family, he said to himself, remembering Gerti Giggles's words. *Remember one thing, everyone's your family*.

Then he flashed back to the note that he

received from Romero. "Call me if you need anything. I'll be right there."

Turning to Carmen, Juni smiled. "Call in *everyone*!" he said.

Within moments, everyone responded. Floop, Minion, Floop's Spy Kids, and the Thumb Thumbs.

"We're here to save the day," proclaimed Floop.

Carmen tossed glasses onto Floop and Minion. Floop got one pair, Minion got four.

"Robot children! Take 'em down!" shouted Minion.

The robot kids' eyes adjusted. They didn't need glasses, and could already see everything. They flew off to attack the robots.

Juni turned and saw someone else approaching. "Dinky Winks!" he shouted happily. Dinky Winks came swooping down with a parachute made out of Troublemaker theme park balloons.

"Did somebody ring the Dinkster?" he asked.

Juni tossed him the glasses, which Dinky put on with a flourish. He saw the robots and nodded happily. "Now *that* would be a nice addition to my park," he said. "Game Over for you, Robotico. Game Over, bud!"

He removed his hat and flung it like a Frisbee. It whacked the robot, and returned to Dinky's head. Dinky then used a rope to hog-tie the robot. He rode it like a bucking bronco.

Gregorio, still caught in the robot's grip, grabbed its arm and saw a cockpit embedded into the architecture of the robot. The arm was actually shaped like a rocket!

"Ingrid! Machete! Felix!" he cried, pointing to the rocket arm, rocket leg, and shoulder.

"Way ahead of you, honey," Ingrid called back. She, Helga, Felix, and Machete all climbed into the robots' built-in rockets. Gregorio reached over and fired up the machine.

"Let's go," said Gregorio. He hit a button and the machine fired up. The robot looked down in shock and disbelief as his arm, leg, and shoulder came apart, turning into manned rockets. Everyone blasted off, leaving the robot suspended in midair for a split second, totally limbless.

Then the robot's giant hand fell, almost crushing Floop. Floop ducked and ended up trapped underneath it.

The Thumb Thumbs flipped the hand over, and Floop and Minion jumped aboard the rocket hand. The Thumbs hung on as Floop drove the giant robot hand like a car.

Just then a flying pig landed nearby. Romero flipped off its back. His cape billowed dramatically behind him.

"Somebody call in a loon?" he asked.

Carmen stepped forward with the last pair of

glasses. "Sorry, Romero," she said. "This is the only pair we have. A little damaged."

Romero removed his cracked glasses and replaced them with the new pair of cracked glasses.

"They're perfect," he said. Then he saw what he was up against. He nodded knowingly. "Oh . . . that's one big experiment gone wrong," he said. He did a back flip onto his winged pig. "Charge, Sporky!" he cried.

Carmen and Juni battled away. Everything was going well until suddenly they both were grabbed by two smaller robots. *Yikes!*

Carmen struggled and managed to talk into her wrist. "Gary Giggles?" she said.

"Yes," replied Gary. He spoke from a ceremony. He was just about to be presented with an award.

"Carmen Cortez," she answered. "I need your help. Right now."

"I'm there," said Gary. He blasted up into the air. The person about to put the medal around his neck stared in shock, the gold medal dangling from his hands.

Shortly, Gary landed near Carmen.

"I'm here!" he said.

"Good, give me a hand." She swung her head and the glasses went flying off her face and onto Gary's. When he put them on he could see what was holding her. He held down the robot while Carmen did some amazing kick-punch-kick combos. The robot was defeated.

"Thanks," said Carmen.

"Don't mention it," replied Gary.

Juni, however, was unable to get to his watch.

"Somebody!" he called.

Just then Gerti landed beside him, her pigtail propellers spinning. She wore goggles.

"I see you called in everyone but me," she said. She reached out and grabbed the robot's ear and twisted it. It cried out in metallic pain. Liberated, Juni turned around and finished off the robot. "How did you know?" he asked.

"My parents called," Gerti told him, pointing. "They're over there, beating up robots."

Juni hopped down. Everyone had their robots under control. Gerti landed next to him.

"Thank you, Gerti," said Juni, holding out his hand. "For everything."

Gerti rolled her eyes at him. "Mushy, mushy, mushy, mushy," she complained. "There's still one more, champ."

They both looked up to see the biggest robot of all, striding down the street. It made all the others looks like mere windup toys.

Everyone stared in disbelief.

"That's . . . impossible," said Gregorio.

"Someone has to go up there," said Ingrid.

"And shut it down manually," added Carmen.

"It's the only way," Juni agreed. "But who?"

Valentin rolled forward. "I'm ready."

Everyone stared at him in silence.

"It must be done," Valentin said levelly. He blasted off.

"Grandpa! No!" Juni shouted.

Ingrid grabbed Juni, holding him back. "Juni, let him go," she said softly. He turned to her, confused.

"Your grandpa has to do this," she explained, taking his hand. They both looked up.

Valentin swooped around the enormous robot like a chopper fighting King Kong. The robot swatted at him and tried to squash him, but Valentin deftly maneuvered away from him, always keeping just out of the robot's reach. Then he flew right into the robot's massive ear.

And there, inside the robot's brain, sat the Toymaker. He was at a control desk, operating the robot.

"Thank you for breaking me free, Valentin," said the Toymaker. "But it's too late. No one can stop me." He turned around and faced his enemy.

"Not even you," he added.

"I know," Valentin admitted. "Only you can do that."

He looked around. The Toymaker's machine was faulty. Pieces began to fall. It was obvious that it wouldn't last much longer.

"You double-crossed us," said Valentin. "The agency, your fellow agents . . . and me. Your mistake cost me my legs. A mistake like that could only push someone further into the dark. And it has. Look at you now."

"But I gave you back your legs when you were in the game!" the Toymaker shouted. "I did that for *you*!"

Valentin shook his head. "Let me tell you all of the things that I missed in my life because of the accident you caused. . . ."

As Valentin began to list the ways his life had been forever altered, the Toymaker's eyes filled with tears. It was nearly unbearable for him to hear what he had done to his old friend and comrade. Valentin finished. The Toymaker was visibly shaken.

"Now," continued Valentin, "let me tell you all the good things that came of it."

This list was so inspirational and insightful that the Toymaker began to smile.

"I only dreamed you would ever say something like that," he said, his voice cracking with emotion.

"We are who we are," Valentin explained. "I

learned to heal, not hurt. To forgive and forget. And that we have to live with that. Work with that . . . make life the best it can be." He backed his chair up. "You've been living in fear of me all these years, but I've only been searching for you so I could tell you . . ." He took a deep breath. "That I forgive you."

The Toymaker slowly lifted his head. He was no longer scared.

"The question is now," said Valentin, "can you forgive yourself? We can stay here and perish. Or leave and start new lives. It's never too late, Sebastian."

The giant robot continued to crumble.

"Take your time to decide," said Valentin. "We have about . . . ten seconds."

The Toymaker stretched out a shaky hand toward a big switch. He reached out and switched it—OFF.

Juni watched the giant robot, hardly daring to breathe. He wondered and worried about what was going on inside the massive creature. Then the robot began to crack. Juni broke away from his mother.

"Juni!" called Mom.

"Grandpa!" Juni cried, as the robot began to crumble around him. "Grandpa!"

"Juni, get out of there!" shouted Gregorio. The robot fell, just missing Juni. Gregorio caught Juni in his arms. Juni grabbed his necklace to take a look. The light was out.

"Juni, look," Gregorio said softly. Juni looked. The necklace was glowing!

Juni ran to the fallen robot just as Valentin wheeled out of it, swinging his necklace. He smiled at his grandson.

Carmen and Juni saluted their grandfather. The Toymaker emerged and stood by Valentin's side. Two old comrades, turned enemies, now comrades again.

Donnagon stared at the scene, confused,

"Wait a minute," he said. "Who won?"

Cesca stepped on his foot.

"It's not whether you win or lose," said Valentin, "but how you play the game." He looked out at the big extended family his grandchildren had called together. He held out his hand.

"To family!" he said.

"To family," everyone repeated, placing their hands on top of his. Juni placed his hand on the big pile.

"To family," Gerti repeated, placing her hand on top of Juni's hand. She winked.

And Juni winked right back.